# Disney's
# THE LITTLE MERMAID

First Edition

1 3 5 7 9 10 8 6 4 2

Library of Congress Catalog Card Number: 92-74259
ISBN: 1-56282-429-5 / 1-56282-430-9 (lib. bdg.)

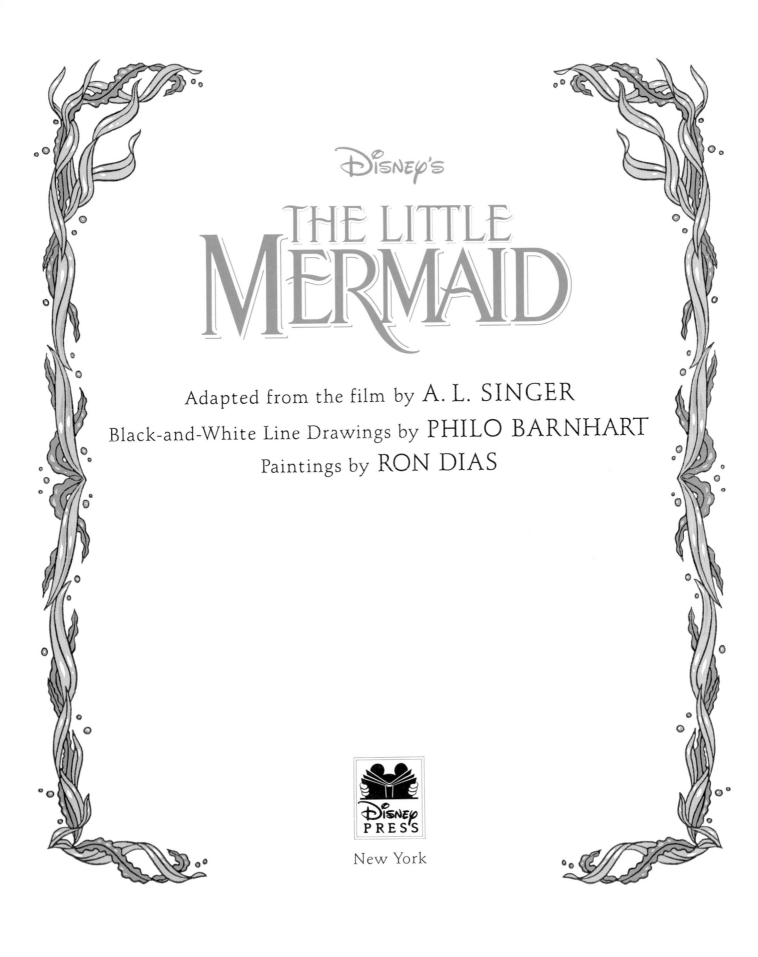

# DISNEY's
# THE LITTLE
# MERMAID

Adapted from the film by A. L. SINGER

Black-and-White Line Drawings by PHILO BARNHART

Paintings by RON DIAS

Disney
PRESS

New York

Heave-ho!" The crew aboard the fine three-masted ship grunted as they pulled up a net filled with fish. It was all in a hard day's work at sea.

A young prince named Eric stood at the railing and lifted his face to the sea air. His faithful sheepdog, Max, stood by his side. The salty wind brushed back Eric's dark hair, and he smiled. The sea was his first love, and he could think of no better place to spend his birthday.

Eric gazed up into the thick clouds. "Isn't this great?" he said. "The salty sea air, the wind blowing in your face. A perfect day to be at sea!"

Near Eric, a gangly older man was bent over the railing. Slowly he raised himself. "Oh, yes," he said, his face green with seasickness. "Delightful." With a groan, he leaned over the side again.

Eric chuckled to himself. Old Grimsby had been his manservant for years, but he had never developed his sea legs.

"A fine strong wind and a following sea!" a sailor called out. "King Triton must be in a friendly mood."

"King Triton?" Eric asked, rushing over to help tie down a sail.

A crusty sailor named Sea Dog piped up, "Why, he's ruler of the merpeople, lad. Thought every good sailor knew about him."

"Hmph! Merpeople!" Grimsby said. "Eric, pay no attention to this nautical nonsense."

Sea Dog frowned. "But it ain't nonsense," he insisted, shaking a fish in Grimsby's face. "It's the truth! They're half fish and half human. I'm telling you, they live down in the depths of the ocean."

Eric had heard this argument many times before. Sea Dog and some of the other sailors were convinced that mer-people existed. Grimsby was absolutely certain they did

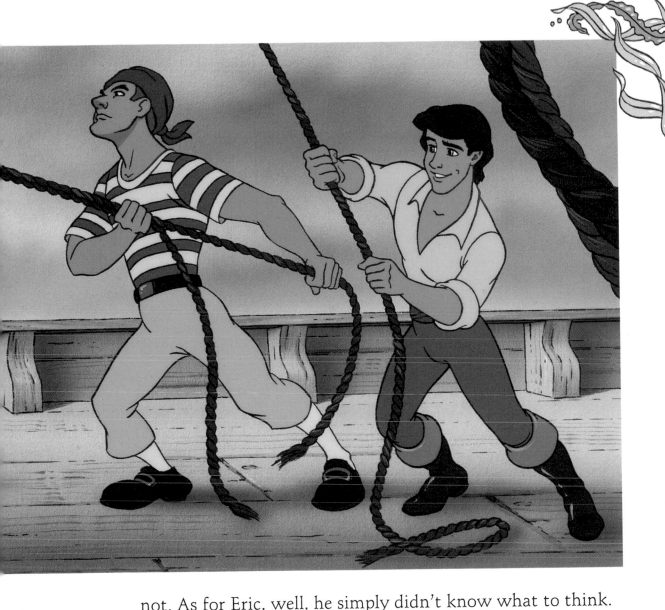

not. As for Eric, well, he simply didn't know what to think.

But if Eric could see to the bottom of the ocean, then he would know *exactly* what to think. For there, fathoms below Eric's ship, was the bustling kingdom of Atlantia. Merpeople and all the other creatures of the deep lived there—far away from human eyes—in a world all their own, a world presided over by the just and noble King Triton.

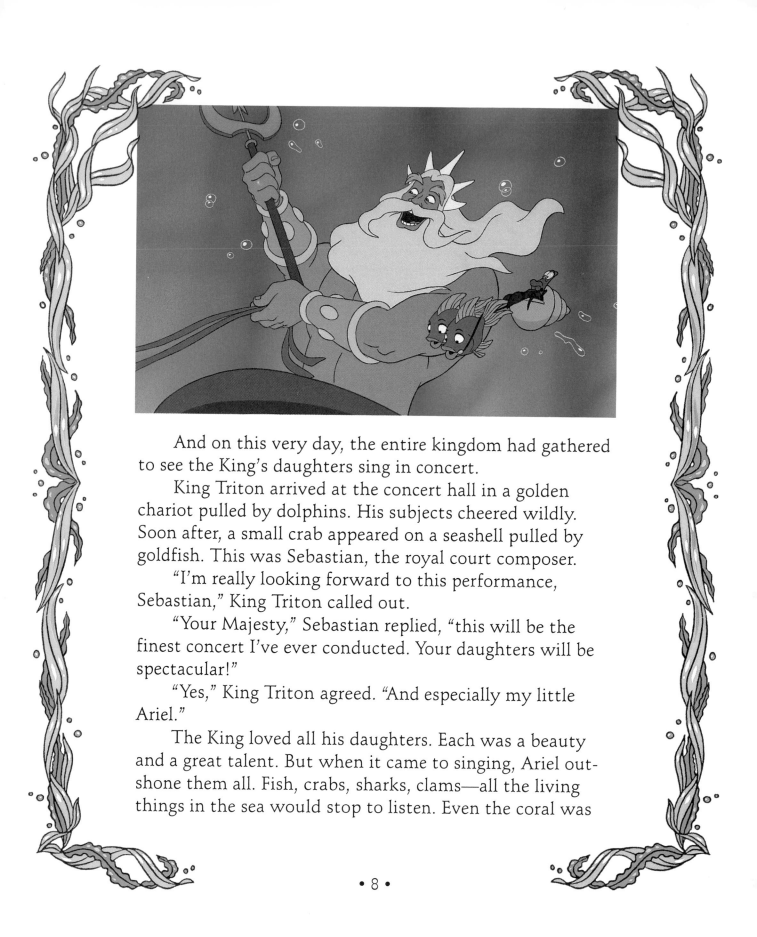

And on this very day, the entire kingdom had gathered to see the King's daughters sing in concert.

King Triton arrived at the concert hall in a golden chariot pulled by dolphins. His subjects cheered wildly. Soon after, a small crab appeared on a seashell pulled by goldfish. This was Sebastian, the royal court composer.

"I'm really looking forward to this performance, Sebastian," King Triton called out.

"Your Majesty," Sebastian replied, "this will be the finest concert I've ever conducted. Your daughters will be spectacular!"

"Yes," King Triton agreed. "And especially my little Ariel."

The King loved all his daughters. Each was a beauty and a great talent. But when it came to singing, Ariel outshone them all. Fish, crabs, sharks, clams—all the living things in the sea would stop to listen. Even the coral was said to sigh with pleasure at the sound of Ariel's singing.

"Ah, Ariel has the most beautiful voice!" Sebastian agreed. But as he rode toward the podium, he grumbled to himself, "If only she'd show up for rehearsals once in a while."

Ariel always seemed to have something better to do than attend her music lessons. And when she did show up, she was late more often than not. But with a big apology, a winning smile, *and* her lovely voice, it was hard for Sebastian to stay angry at her. As for where she had been keeping herself, nobody knew.

Sebastian climbed the podium. When he raised his baton, an orchestra of fish musicians lifted their instruments. An octopus drummer became poised with his drumsticks.

Down came the baton, and the musicians began to play. A curtain of bubbles rose upward. Three huge clamshells appeared on the stage. They opened to reveal six mermaids, all daughters of King Triton—Aquata, Andrina, Arista, Attina, Adella, and Alana.

As they swam around, singing sweetly, another closed clamshell swirled onto the stage. Everyone knew that Ariel was inside—and they couldn't wait to hear her sing.

Slowly, with all eyes upon it, the shell opened, and there, in the middle, stood…no one. The shell was empty.

The sisters stopped singing. Sebastian dropped his baton. The audience gasped in shocked surprise.

King Triton rose from his seat, clenching his trident. His face turned red with fury as he let out a bellow that shook the seafloor.

"Ariel!"

# CHAPTER TWO

Ariel glided through the water at top speed. With each tail stroke, her red hair swept back like a thick flame. In her right hand she clutched a sturdy, empty sack. In a few minutes the sack would be filled with fascinating things—things from the world above the water. She couldn't wait.

Ariel stopped swimming when she reached an old shipwreck. The ship's rotting hull was covered with seaweed and barnacles, and the mast was broken in two. Through the portholes Ariel could see a glimpse of the dark and eerie interior.

To Ariel this was the most beautiful sight in the sea. A shipwreck was mysterious, exotic. It was from that *other* world.

Merpeople were forbidden to go above the water. It was King Triton's strictest rule—and one that Ariel just could not obey. Whenever she could, Ariel would sneak up to the surface to look around. She'd even made friends with a sea gull named Scuttle.

Ariel was curious about everything above the surface, especially the land creatures called humans. She knew her father's rule was designed to keep his subjects—including his daughters—from interacting with humans. King Triton said that these land creatures were dangerous and could not be trusted. Ariel had never seen any humans up close before, but she didn't understand how, if they could make all the beautiful things she had collected from the ocean floor, they could be so evil.

"Isn't this ship fantastic?" Ariel called over her shoulder.

"Yeah, sure," answered a small roly-poly fish, huffing and puffing to keep up with her. His name was Flounder, and he was Ariel's best friend.

He was not only terribly out of breath, he was scared, too.

"Uh, let's get out of here, Ariel," Flounder said. "It looks damp in there. And I think I may be coming down with a cough."

"Well, I'm going inside," Ariel said. "You can just stay here and watch for sharks."

Ariel swam through a porthole. "Sharks?" Flounder squeaked. "*Ariel, wait!*"

Flipping his fins wildly, Flounder headed right into the porthole—and got stuck. "Ariel, help!" he called out, twisting himself right and left.

Inside the ship, at the top of a staircase, Ariel turned. "Oh, Flounder...." Laughing, she swam back toward him.

Flounder shook with fear. "Ariel," he whispered, "do you really think there might be sharks around here?"

"Flounder, don't be such a guppy," Ariel said.

"I'm not a guppy!"

*Thoonk!* With a strong yank, Ariel pulled her friend into the ship.

Flounder stayed close to Ariel. The darkness frightened him. In every corner he saw strange, shadowy shapes. And he had an uneasy feeling that he and Ariel were being watched.

Ariel and Flounder swam up, through a hole in the ceiling, to the next level of the ship. There, on a pile of broken boards, lay a shiny, dented fork. Ariel gasped with delight and quickly swam over to seize it.

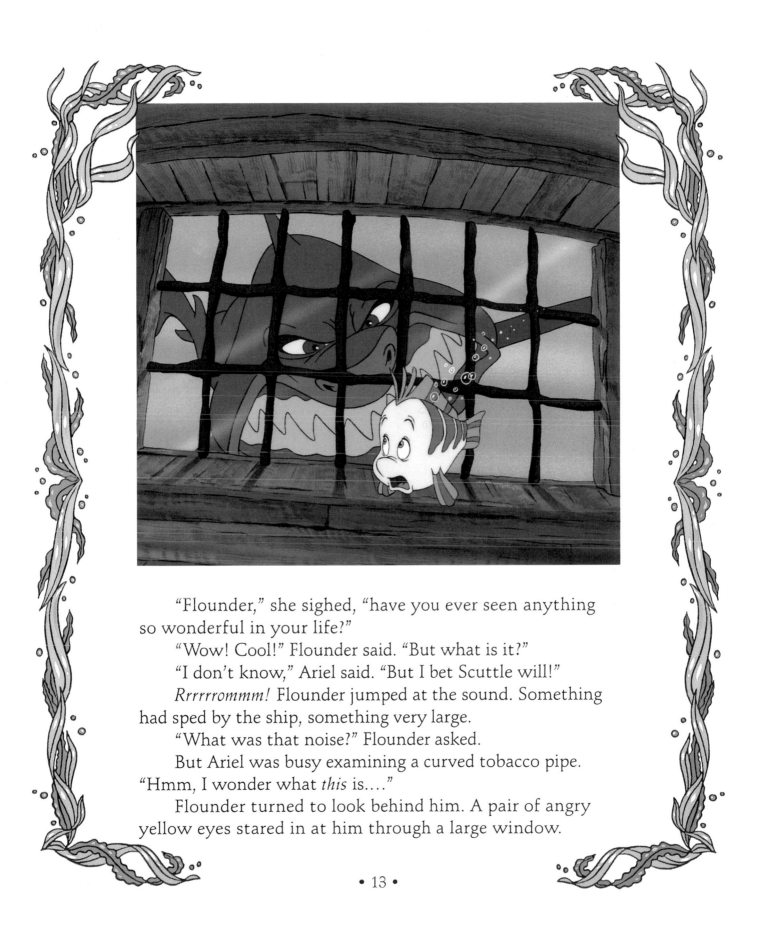

"Flounder," she sighed, "have you ever seen anything so wonderful in your life?"

"Wow! Cool!" Flounder said. "But what is it?"

"I don't know," Ariel said. "But I bet Scuttle will!"

*Rrrrrrommm!* Flounder jumped at the sound. Something had sped by the ship, something very large.

"What was that noise?" Flounder asked.

But Ariel was busy examining a curved tobacco pipe. "Hmm, I wonder what *this* is...."

Flounder turned to look behind him. A pair of angry yellow eyes stared in at him through a large window.

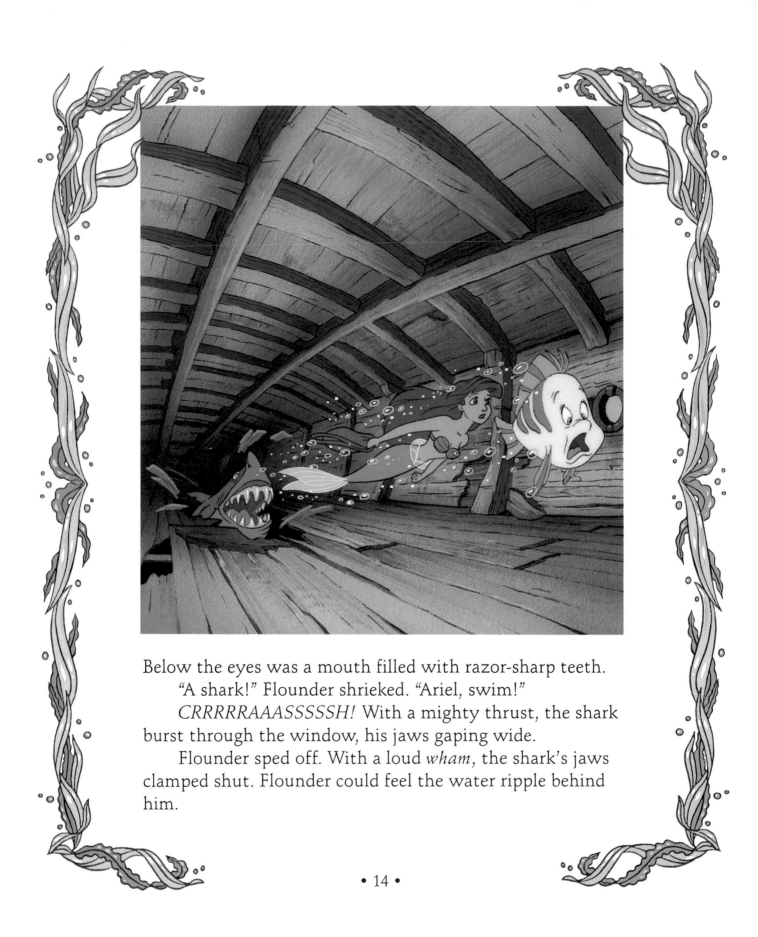

Below the eyes was a mouth filled with razor-sharp teeth.

"A shark!" Flounder shrieked. "Ariel, swim!"

*CRRRRRAAASSSSSH!* With a mighty thrust, the shark burst through the window, his jaws gaping wide.

Flounder sped off. With a loud *wham*, the shark's jaws clamped shut. Flounder could feel the water ripple behind him.

Ariel quickly threw the pipe into her sack. She and Flounder darted up to the next floor. They raced away, over broken wooden planks that jutted up from below.

Suddenly Ariel felt herself being jerked backward. She looked down in horror.

Her bag was stuck on a plank. Quickly she grabbed it and, just inches ahead of the shark, swam for her life. She and Flounder swam out of the ship and went spiraling up around the mast of another.

*Bonk!* In his panic Flounder banged into the mast. The blow stunned him, and he sank slowly down toward the ocean floor.

Ariel sped to catch her friend before the shark did. She reached through the ring of an enormous anchor and snatched Flounder just inches from the ground.

With the shark advancing rapidly toward them, Ariel and Flounder popped back through the ring. Flounder had now recovered from his blow, and he and Ariel swam off as quickly as they could.

The speeding shark was concentrating so hard on his prey that he swam straight into the ring, where his neck became stuck tight. He wriggled angrily, but the ring held fast.

Flounder, sensing that the danger had now passed, turned back and stuck out his tongue. "You big bully!" The shark growled with fury, and Flounder recoiled in fear.

Ariel couldn't help chuckling. "Flounder, you really *are* a guppy," she said.

"I am not!" Flounder protested as the two friends made their way up to the surface.

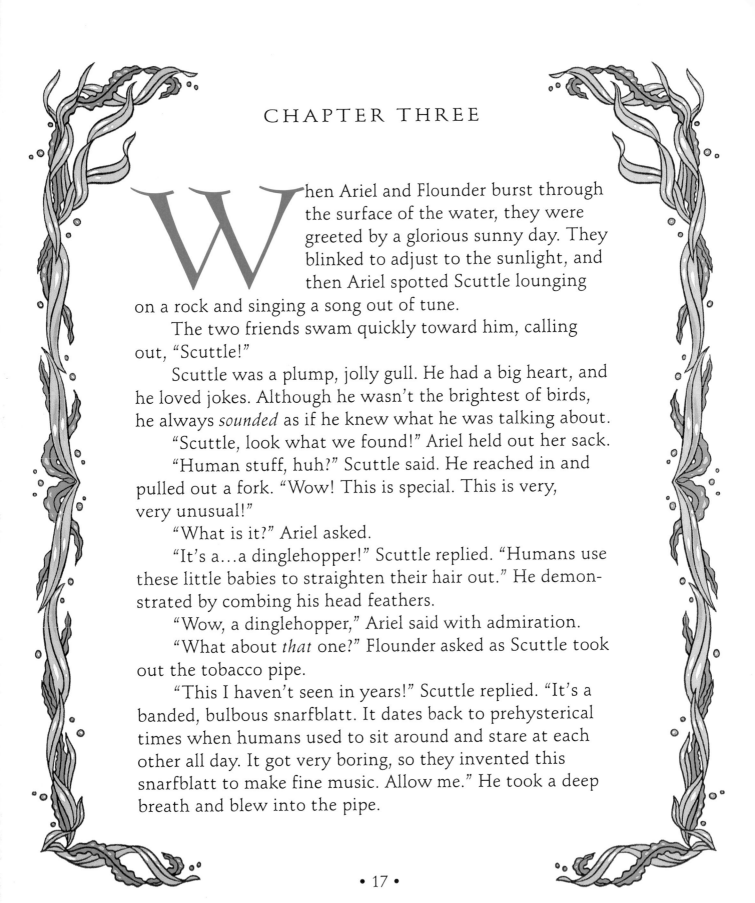

## CHAPTER THREE

When Ariel and Flounder burst through the surface of the water, they were greeted by a glorious sunny day. They blinked to adjust to the sunlight, and then Ariel spotted Scuttle lounging on a rock and singing a song out of tune.

The two friends swam quickly toward him, calling out, "Scuttle!"

Scuttle was a plump, jolly gull. He had a big heart, and he loved jokes. Although he wasn't the brightest of birds, he always *sounded* as if he knew what he was talking about.

"Scuttle, look what we found!" Ariel held out her sack.

"Human stuff, huh?" Scuttle said. He reached in and pulled out a fork. "Wow! This is special. This is very, very unusual!"

"What is it?" Ariel asked.

"It's a...a dinglehopper!" Scuttle replied. "Humans use these little babies to straighten their hair out." He demonstrated by combing his head feathers.

"Wow, a dinglehopper," Ariel said with admiration.

"What about *that* one?" Flounder asked as Scuttle took out the tobacco pipe.

"This I haven't seen in years!" Scuttle replied. "It's a banded, bulbous snarfblatt. It dates back to prehysterical times when humans used to sit around and stare at each other all day. It got very boring, so they invented this snarfblatt to make fine music. Allow me." He took a deep breath and blew into the pipe.

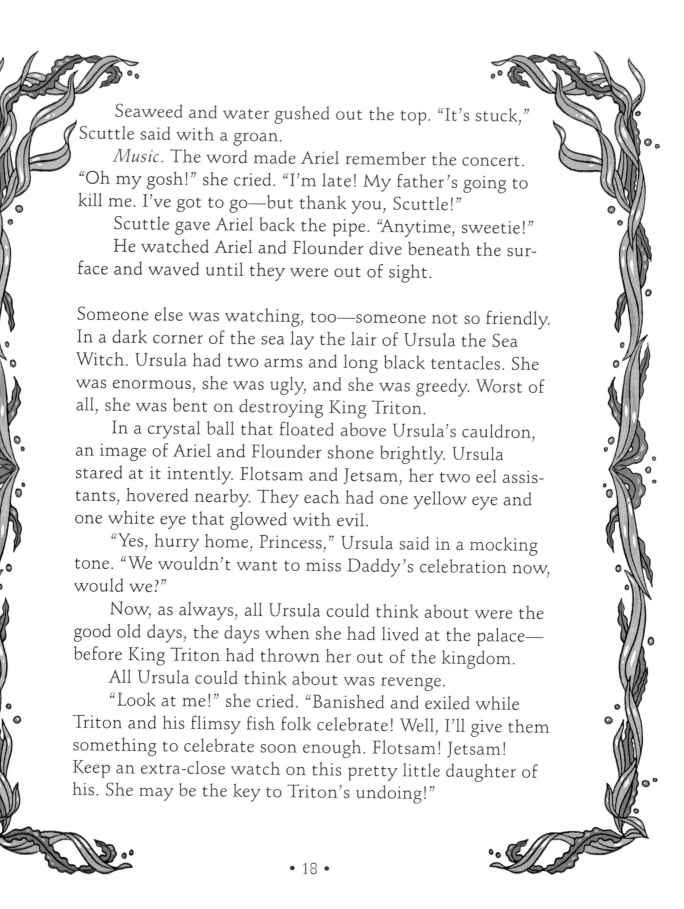

Seaweed and water gushed out the top. "It's stuck," Scuttle said with a groan.

*Music*. The word made Ariel remember the concert. "Oh my gosh!" she cried. "I'm late! My father's going to kill me. I've got to go—but thank you, Scuttle!"

Scuttle gave Ariel back the pipe. "Anytime, sweetie!"

He watched Ariel and Flounder dive beneath the surface and waved until they were out of sight.

Someone else was watching, too—someone not so friendly. In a dark corner of the sea lay the lair of Ursula the Sea Witch. Ursula had two arms and long black tentacles. She was enormous, she was ugly, and she was greedy. Worst of all, she was bent on destroying King Triton.

In a crystal ball that floated above Ursula's cauldron, an image of Ariel and Flounder shone brightly. Ursula stared at it intently. Flotsam and Jetsam, her two eel assistants, hovered nearby. They each had one yellow eye and one white eye that glowed with evil.

"Yes, hurry home, Princess," Ursula said in a mocking tone. "We wouldn't want to miss Daddy's celebration now, would we?"

Now, as always, all Ursula could think about were the good old days, the days when she had lived at the palace— before King Triton had thrown her out of the kingdom.

All Ursula could think about was revenge.

"Look at me!" she cried. "Banished and exiled while Triton and his flimsy fish folk celebrate! Well, I'll give them something to celebrate soon enough. Flotsam! Jetsam! Keep an extra-close watch on this pretty little daughter of his. She may be the key to Triton's undoing!"

# CHAPTER FOUR

Ariel stood before her father in the throne room, her head bowed slightly while he scolded her for missing the concert. Flounder hid behind the throne room door.

"I just don't know what we're going to do with you, young lady," the King bellowed, the disappointment in his voice clear. "As a result of your careless behavior, the entire celebration was—"

Suddenly his flowing white beard parted. Sebastian peered out and said, "Ruined! It was ruined! Completely destroyed. This concert was to be the pinnacle of my entire career. Now, thanks to you, I am the laughingstock of the entire kingdom!"

Flounder hated to hear Ariel being yelled at. Before he could even think to stop himself, he swam toward the throne.

"It wasn't her fault!" he cried out, suddenly aware that he now had the full attention of both Sebastian and the King. He was instantly nervous. "Well, um, first this shark chased us, but we got away. Then there was this sea gull, and—"

"*Sea gull?*" King Triton bellowed.

Whoops. Flounder quickly hid behind Ariel.

"You went up to the surface again, didn't you?" King Triton said. "How many times must we go through this? You could have been seen by one of those barbarians, by one of those humans! Do you think I want my youngest daughter to be snared by some fish-eater's hook?"

"But Daddy, I'm sixteen years old," Ariel began in her defense. "I'm not a child anymore!"

"Don't you take that tone of voice with me, young lady," the King thundered. "As long as you live under *my* ocean, you'll observe *my* rules!"

"But if you would only listen—"

"Not another word! And you are *never* to go to the surface again. Is that clear?"

Ariel tried to stare at her father to show him that she wouldn't back down. But it was no use. She could feel her lip start to quiver and her eyes start to tear. She turned and swam out of the throne room, with Flounder following close behind.

King Triton sighed. It was not easy being tough on his daughters; he loved them so dearly.

"Do you think I was too hard on her?" he asked Sebastian.

"Definitely not!" Sebastian replied. "These teenagers, they think they know everything. You give them an inch, they swim all over you! Why, if Ariel were my daughter, I'd show her who was boss. None of this flitting to the surface and other such nonsense. No, sir, I'd keep her under tight control!"

King Triton sat back. Sebastian was giving him an idea. "You know, you're absolutely right, Sebastian," he said. "Ariel needs constant supervision."

"Constant!" Sebastian echoed.

"Someone to watch over her, to keep her out of trouble."

"All the time!"

"And you are just the crab to do it!"

Sebastian froze. That was not what he had in mind. Taking care of Ariel would be a full-time job. He was the royal court composer, not a baby-sitter. But he knew there would be no arguing with the King. When the King asked you to do something, you did it.

Sebastian sank into his shell. Muttering to himself, he swam away from the King's chamber and out into the ocean, where he caught sight of Ariel and Flounder. They were looking around suspiciously—as if they didn't want to be followed.

"Hmm," Sebastian said. "I wonder what that girl is up to now." He swam off behind Ariel and Flounder, hiding in the shadows.

The two friends came to a rock wall in front of which

a large boulder was lodged. With a grunt and some effort, Ariel pushed the boulder aside.

Sebastian gasped. Behind the huge rock was the opening to a dark grotto. Ariel and Flounder disappeared inside.

Thrusting his tiny legs forward as quickly as he could, Sebastian raced in after them. He hid in a corner and looked around in wonder.

The cave was enormous. It rose so high Sebastian couldn't see the ceiling. On the shelflike crags in the walls he could make out small objects: vases, plates, books, clocks, candle holders, eyeglasses, a harp. Sebastian had never seen such things, but he knew they must have come from the human world.

"Oh, Flounder," Ariel said, sitting gloomily on the cave floor. "If only I could make Father understand. I just don't see things the way he does. I don't see how a world that makes such wonderful things could be so bad." She swam upward, admiring all her treasures. "What I wouldn't give to see what the human world is like!"

Sebastian was listening so intently to Ariel that he backed right into a beer stein. With a *thunk*, the top swung shut and the stein fell over and rolled off the edge of a crag. It bumped down the wall and crashed onto the cave floor.

"Sebastian!" Ariel cried in shock.

Sebastian lay in a tangle of knickknacks. "Ariel, what is all this?" he said as he stood up quickly.

"It's just my collection," Ariel replied.

"If your father knew about this place, he'd—"

"You're not going to tell him, are you?" Flounder asked.

"Oh, please, Sebastian," Ariel pleaded. "He would never understand."

Sebastian took Ariel's hand and began pulling her toward the cavern's entrance. "You're under a lot of pressure down here, Princess," he said. "Come with me. I'll take you home and get you something warm to drink."

Ariel felt a shadow pass over them. She looked up at the small opening, way above them, at the top of the cave.

"Hmm, what do you suppose *that* is?" Ariel murmured. She slipped out of Sebastian's grip and swam upward.

"Ariel!" Sebastian screamed, and swam after her. He could hardly believe that after everything that had just happened, the little mermaid was heading for the surface again!

# CHAPTER FIVE

Sebastian was furious. He certainly had no business being above the water. And there were Ariel and Flounder, just bobbing in the water, looking at something straight ahead of them.

"Ariel," Sebastian said, demanding an explanation. "What are you—"

KABOOOOM! An explosion cut Sebastian off. He turned around and gasped in shock. A large three-masted ship lay anchored in the water close by. Fireworks from the ship lit up the night sky in bright colors, their sparks floating gently down to the water.

The next thing Sebastian knew, Ariel was swimming toward the ship. She ignored his calls to return at once, as she was so intent on seeing what was happening on board.

Ariel peeked through an opening in the side of the ship, hidden by the darkness. She watched as a shipful of sailors in striped shirts and brown trousers laughed and sang and danced.

What fantastic things their legs were! she thought. The men used them to leap, skip, jump, and dance.

Barbarians? Was that what her father had called humans? They sure didn't look that way to Ariel.

There was a shaggy, furry creature on board that barked and jumped around on four legs. When it saw Ariel, it bounded over and licked her face.

"Max!" called a strong voice. "Here, boy!"

The dog leapt happily over to one of the young men.

The man laughed, and his cheeks dimpled. His dark hair fell across his forehead as he lifted a fife to his mouth.

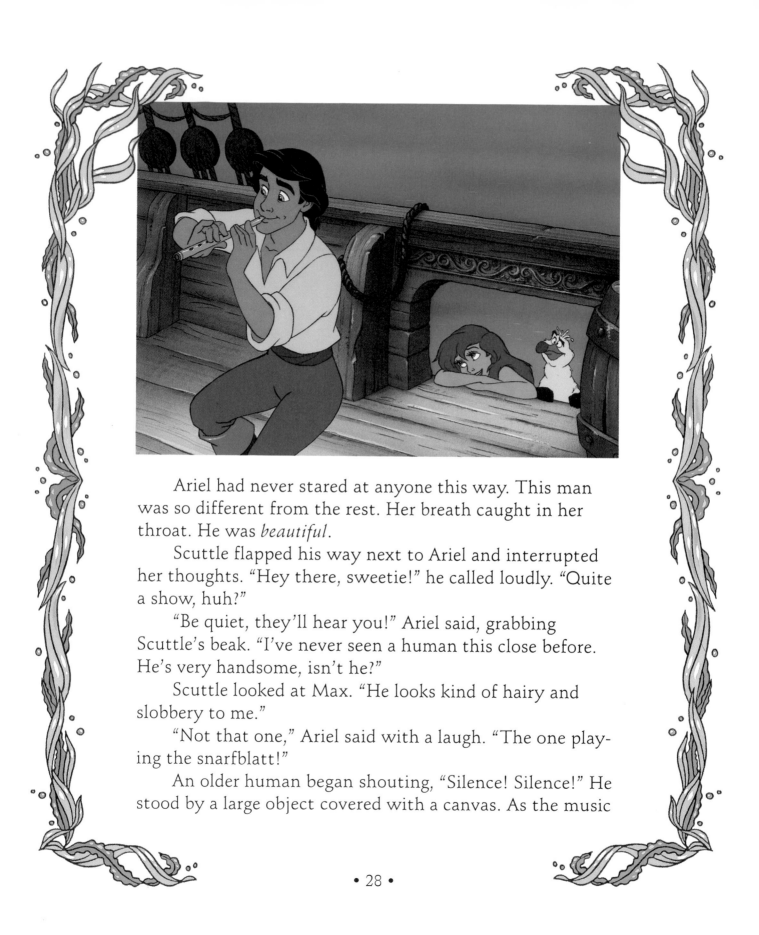

Ariel had never stared at anyone this way. This man was so different from the rest. Her breath caught in her throat. He was *beautiful*.

Scuttle flapped his way next to Ariel and interrupted her thoughts. "Hey there, sweetie!" he called loudly. "Quite a show, huh?"

"Be quiet, they'll hear you!" Ariel said, grabbing Scuttle's beak. "I've never seen a human this close before. He's very handsome, isn't he?"

Scuttle looked at Max. "He looks kind of hairy and slobbery to me."

"Not that one," Ariel said with a laugh. "The one playing the snarfblatt!"

An older human began shouting, "Silence! Silence!" He stood by a large object covered with a canvas. As the music fizzled out, the older man announced, "It is now my honor and privilege to present our esteemed Prince Eric with a very special, very expensive, very large birthday present."

"Hurrah!" shouted the men. Some of them clapped the handsome sailor on the back.

Ariel leaned forward to listen.

Prince Eric blushed and said, "Ah, Grimsby, you ol' beanpole, you shouldn't have!"

He's humble, too, Ariel thought. She liked that.

With a smile, Grimsby pulled off the canvas sheet. It fell to the deck, revealing a statue of Eric underneath.

All the sailors applauded. Grimsby looked proud of himself. But Eric thought that while the *face* on the statue looked like his, the pose certainly wasn't him. This figure looked the part of a conquering hero. His chest was puffed out with pride, he gripped a sword in his hand, and he looked about to scramble up a rock.

"Gee, Grim, it's…uh, it's really something," Eric managed to say.

"Well, I had hoped it would be a wedding present, but…"

Eric chuckled. "Come on, Grim, don't start that again."

"Oh, Eric," Grimsby said with a sigh. "It isn't me alone. The entire kingdom wants to see you happily settled down with the right girl."

Eric walked to the railing and looked out to sea. Ariel followed him with her eyes, hypnotized. "Oh, she's out there somewhere. Believe me, Grim, when I find her, I'll know. It'll just hit me, like lightning."

*BOOOOOM!* As if on cue, a thunderclap sounded, and lightning bathed the ship in harsh light. "Hurricane a-coming!" a sailor shouted. "Stand fast; secure the rigging!"

The crew leapt into action. They quickly tied down the sails and ropes. A huge wave rose over the ship, crashing over Ariel's head. A few yards behind her, Flounder and Sebastian disappeared under the water. Scuttle flapped his wings, but the wind forced him backward. "Ariel!" he shouted.

Ariel tried to hold on to the ship, but it was impossible. She plunged into the sea, head over tail. Struggling against the current, she fought her way upward.

She got back to the surface just in time to see a crack of lightning strike the ship. Instantly the mainsail went up in flames.

Ariel watched in horror as the flames spread. She saw Eric at the steering wheel, trying to guide the ship away from a sharp outcropping of rocks.

*CRASH!* With a sickening sound, the ship's hull bashed into the rocks. Sailors slid across the deck. Eric lost his balance. He hurtled into Grimsby. Flailing their arms, they both fell overboard.

They landed near a rowboat that the first mate had cut loose from the ship. "Grim, hang on!" Eric shouted. He hopped aboard the rowboat and pulled Grimsby in after him.

*"Arf! Arf!"*

Above the roaring tempest, Eric heard Max's bark. His eyes darted toward the ship. It was engulfed in fire—and Max was trapped.

Eric dove overboard and swam against the raging sea. Gasping for breath, he finally reached the burning ship and climbed aboard.

"Max!" Eric called, pulling himself up on deck.

*CRRRAAACK!* Above Eric, the mainmast broke. It tumbled downward, burning like a mammoth torch. Flames immediately began to spread right down to the lower deck, where the room holding the fireworks and gunpowder was.

Eric jumped away and looked up to see Max standing on the top of a staircase. He was shaking, afraid to jump.

"Come on, boy!" Eric held out his arms. "Jump!"

Max barked again and looked about fearfully. Finally, on unsteady legs, he jumped into Eric's arms.

Eric ran with Max to the railing, but his foot broke through the wooden deck and became firmly stuck there. The force of the sudden stop caused Eric to toss Max over-

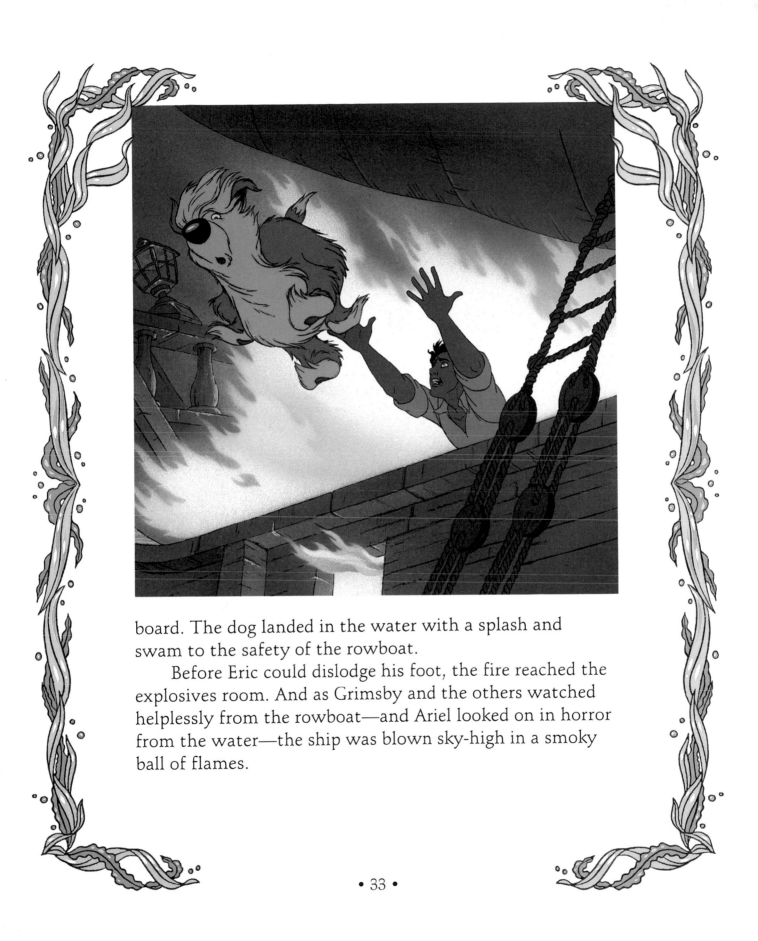

board. The dog landed in the water with a splash and swam to the safety of the rowboat.

Before Eric could dislodge his foot, the fire reached the explosives room. And as Grimsby and the others watched helplessly from the rowboat—and Ariel looked on in horror from the water—the ship was blown sky-high in a smoky ball of flames.

# CHAPTER SIX

Ariel felt as if her heart had stopped. Splinters of wood and pieces of twisted metal were raining down around her. She shielded herself, desperately looking for Eric amid the floating wreckage.

Finally she saw a slumped figure dressed in tattered clothing, clinging to a piece of driftwood. It was Eric. She watched as he slipped off the wood and sank slowly under the water. She swam to him as fast as she could, wrapped her arm around him, and lifted his head above the water. While fireworks exploded all around them, Ariel swam with the unconscious man toward the shore. The waves tossed them up and down. Rain whipped their faces. She wanted so much to swim under the sea, but she had heard that humans could drown. So she just gritted her teeth and kept on going until she reached land.

Scuttle joined Ariel, who sat watching the motionless Prince.

"Is he...dead?" Ariel asked.

Scuttle lifted Eric's bare foot and put it to his ear. "I can't make out a heartbeat."

"No, look, he's breathing," Ariel said. She smiled as Eric let out a small sigh. "He's so beautiful."

Ariel could feel something well up inside her. It was more than joy, more than happiness. A gentle love song formed in her heart, and she began to sing it softly.

Sebastian and Flounder arrived in time to see Eric open his eyes. Sebastian's jaw dropped in shock as Eric blinked and looked straight at Ariel. In his daze and in the glare of the sun he couldn't see her very clearly. But he could hear her song.

And then—"*Arf! Arf!*"—Max came bounding over a sand dune. Barking happily, he jumped on Eric and licked his face.

"Eric!" Grimsby shouted from nearby.

Ariel quickly jumped into the water and swam to a nearby rock, just out of Eric's sight. Sebastian and Flounder followed close behind.

"Eric!" Grimsby said, coming over the dune. "My boy, you do enjoy making me worry, don't you?"

Eric shook his head. He was still dizzy, still not quite conscious. "A girl rescued me…," he mumbled. "She…she was singing. She had the most beautiful voice!"

Grimsby hoisted Eric to his feet. "Ah, Eric, I think you've swallowed a bit too much seawater. Come on now, off we go!"

From her perch Ariel watched them walk over the hill.

"We are going to forget this whole thing ever happened!" Sebastian spoke nervously. "The Sea King will never know. *You* won't tell him. *I* won't tell him. And, I will stay in one piece!"

Ariel wasn't listening. Her mind was still on Eric. He was gone now—over the dune, into a world where she was not allowed. A world of air and trees, of sand and grass; a world of humans.

Someday, she vowed to herself, someday I'll find a way to be part of that world.

Deep in the ocean, Ursula the Sea Witch began to laugh. Her eyes were glued to the crystal ball. In it she could see Ariel. And she recognized the look on the girl's face.

"Oh, it's too easy!" she gloated. "The child is in love with a human. And not just any human—a prince! Her daddy will love that!"

She threw her head back and cackled gleefully. She shot a glance at her garden of shriveled, quivering creatures—her collection of souls. Each ugly mass had once been a merperson, a merperson with a desire so strong he or she had struck up a deal with Ursula. The deal was that Ursula would grant a merperson his or her greatest wish, but the deals always ended not only with unfulfilled dreams but with a place in Ursula's collection. Ursula saw to that.

It was so simple, and so many merpeople fell for it. The more souls Ursula had, the better she liked it.

But the whole collection was nothing compared with what she now had in mind. Her face glowed as she grinned at Ariel's image. "King Triton's headstrong, lovesick girl would make a charming addition to my little garden!" she declared with an evil laugh.

# CHAPTER SEVEN

Her sisters could tell that Ariel was in love. She had that faraway look in her eyes and day-dreamed more than ever. They all assumed she'd fallen for a merman. Only Sebastian and Flounder knew the whole truth.

Sebastian paced the ocean floor, worried sick. Ariel sat on a rock above him, plucking the petals of a yellow sea flower.

"He loves me, he loves me not...," she said.

"Okay. So far, so good," Sebastian said. "I don't think the King knows...but it will not be easy keeping something like this a secret for long!"

"He loves me! I knew it!" Ariel exclaimed as she pulled off the last petal.

"Ariel, stop talking crazy!" Sebastian said.

"I've got to see him again. Tonight! Scuttle knows where he lives. I'll swim up to his castle. Then Flounder will splash around and get his attention. Then we'll—"

"Ariel! Will you get your head out of the clouds and back in the water where it belongs? Down here is your home! The human world, it's a mess. Life under the sea is better than anything they've got up there! Safe and happy. Everything is beautiful. Humans like to put us in bowls, and when they get hungry—ha! Guess who is cooked for dinner?"

Sebastian went on and on, gesturing and pacing. When he looked up, Ariel was gone.

"Ohhh," he said with frustration, "somebody's got to nail that girl's fins to the floor!"

"Sebastian!" a voice called from behind.

Sebastian turned to see a sea horse racing toward him. "I've got an urgent message from the Sea King!" the sea horse announced. "He wants to see you right away. Something about Ariel!"

Sebastian gulped. The King had found out! Sebastian's career was over, he just knew it. He had failed to take care of Ariel. The King would surely banish him—if he were lucky.

Shaking, Sebastian swam toward the castle.

In the throne room King Triton chuckled to himself. Imagine! His youngest daughter in love—and that rascal Sebastian had kept it a secret. Who could the lucky mer-man be? he wondered.

When Sebastian entered, the King decided to tease him a bit. "Uh, Sebastian, I'm concerned about Ariel. Have you noticed she's been acting peculiar lately?"

"Peculiar?" Sebastian asked with a smile.

"You know," said Triton, "mooning about, daydreaming, singing to herself?"

"Oh, ooh, well, I—" Sebastian stammered.

King Triton raised an eyebrow. "Sebastian," he said, "I know you've been keeping something from me."

"K-k-keeping something?"

"About Ariel."

"Ariel?" Sebastian's legs were clattering now.

"Being in love?" King Triton picked up his trident and pointed it playfully at Sebastian. "Hmmm?"

Suddenly Sebastian fell to his knees. He grabbed the King's beard and began to whimper. "I tried to stop her, sir! She wouldn't listen! I told her to stay away from humans! They are bad! They are trouble. They—"

King Triton sat bolt upright. His eyes glowed with
a fiery rage. "*Humans?*" he bellowed. "What about
humans?"

His trident began to glow brightly. He lifted Sebastian
to eye level.

Sebastian gulped. He had a lot of explaining to do.


"Come on!" Flounder called to Ariel as he led her into the
grotto.

"Flounder, why can't you tell me what this is about?"
Ariel pleaded.

"You'll see. It's a surprise!"

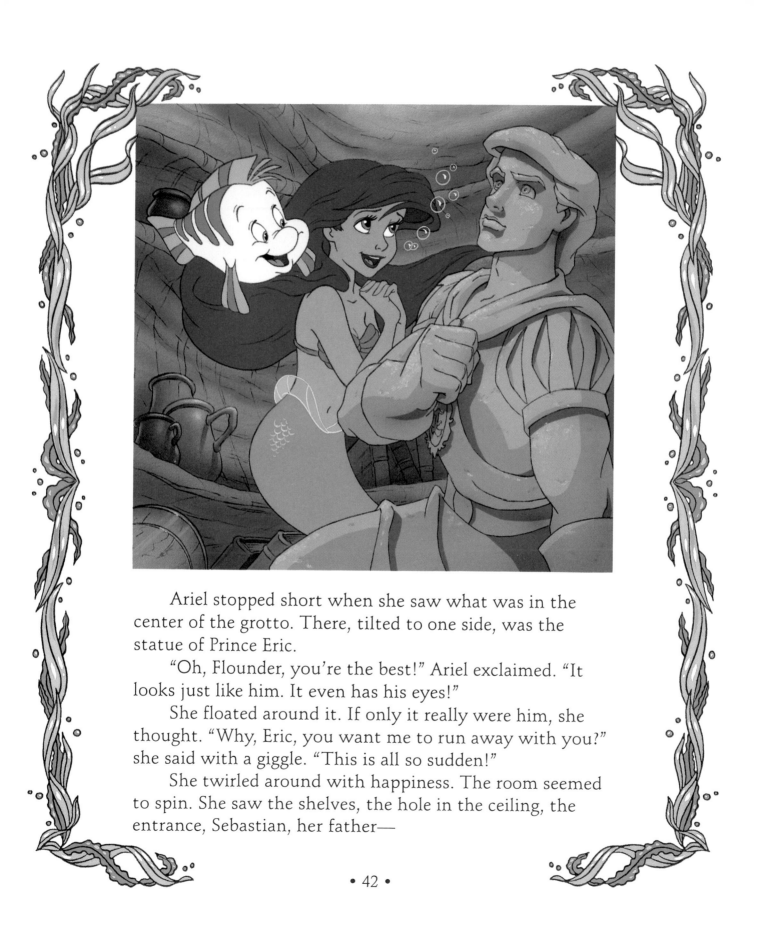

Ariel stopped short when she saw what was in the center of the grotto. There, tilted to one side, was the statue of Prince Eric.

"Oh, Flounder, you're the best!" Ariel exclaimed. "It looks just like him. It even has his eyes!"

She floated around it. If only it really were him, she thought. "Why, Eric, you want me to run away with you?" she said with a giggle. "This is all so sudden!"

She twirled around with happiness. The room seemed to spin. She saw the shelves, the hole in the ceiling, the entrance, Sebastian, her father—

Her father!

"Daddy!" Ariel cried.

Flounder darted behind a large chest. Sebastian began biting his claw nervously.

King Triton stepped out of the entrance and into the grotto. In the uneven light his face was etched in shadows. "I consider myself a reasonable merman. I set certain rules, and I expect those rules to be obeyed," he said sternly. "Is it true you rescued a human from drowning?"

"Daddy, I had to!" Ariel protested.

"Contact between the human world and the merworld is strictly forbidden. Ariel, you know that. Everyone knows that!"

"He would have died!"

"One less human to worry about!" King Triton scowled angrily.

"You don't even know him," Ariel said heatedly.

"Know him?" Triton roared. "I don't have to know him. They're all the same—spineless savage harpooning fish-eaters! Incapable of any feeling or—"

"Daddy, I love him!"

Ariel gasped and put her hands to her mouth. She couldn't believe she admitted that to her father. But it was true, truer than anything she had ever said in her life.

The words hit King Triton like a fist. His jaw dropped in shock. "No! Have you lost your senses completely? He's a human, you're a mermaid!"

"I don't care!" she replied.

"So help me, Ariel, I am going to get through to you," the King said through clenched teeth. "And if this is the only way, so be it!"

His trident began to glow a bright, angry orange. He

lifted it high and pointed it at the shelves filled with objects from the human world.

*WHAM!* A beam of orange light shot from the trident and smashed a candelabra.

*WHAM!* A ceramic globe exploded into bits.

Ariel's face went pale with horror. "Daddy! No!" she screamed.

*WHAM! WHAM! WHAM!* One by one King Triton destroyed object after object. Ariel swam to her father's side. "Stop it! Stop it!" she pleaded.

But the King's eyes were focused on the statue now. That must be the human Ariel loved, he reasoned. That was the one who could threaten the lives of everyone in his kingdom. He pointed the trident directly at it.

"*Daaaddddy!*" Ariel screamed.

*CCRRRRRRAAACCK!* The trident's bolt of energy was enormous. The statue exploded into tiny pieces and fell into all the corners of the grotto.

And that was it. The King gave Ariel another stern glance. Then his trident stopped glowing.

Ariel looked over to where the statue had been. There was now only a flat rock with a few jagged pieces of stone. She put her head down and began to cry.

The King's face softened in sadness at his daughter's unhappiness, and he left the grotto with his head bowed. Slowly Flounder and Sebastian came out of their hiding places. They swam toward Ariel.

"Ariel," Sebastian said softly. "I—"

"Just go away," Ariel replied.

Sebastian nodded. He felt awful. He and Flounder gave each other a look. They knew Ariel needed to be alone so, quietly, with sad faces, they swam away.

Ariel didn't see them go. And she didn't see Flotsam and Jetsam approach, either.

"Poor, sweet child," Flotsam said.

"She has a very serious problem," said Jetsam.

"If only there was something we could do for her."

Flotsam and Jetsam stared at Ariel, trying to look concerned.

Ariel glanced up. She had never seen these two eels before. Their words were kind, but she didn't feel comfortable with them.

"Who are you?" she asked.

"Don't be scared," Flotsam said. "We represent someone who can make all your dreams come true."

"You and your prince," Jetsam added.

"Together forever," they chimed at the same time.

"I—I don't understand," Ariel said warily.

Flotsam grinned. "Ursula has great powers."

"The Sea Witch?" Ariel was filled with disgust. "Why, that's…I couldn't possibly. No! Get out of here! Leave me alone!"

"Suit yourself," Jetsam said, turning to swim away.

"It was only a suggestion." As Flotsam left, he swam over the rubble of Prince Eric's statue. The face was lying there, staring blankly upward. Flotsam flicked it with his tail, and it rolled toward Ariel.

Ariel gently picked up the broken sculpture. It was an amazing likeness.

*Spineless. Savage. Incapable of feeling.* King Triton's words came back to her. How could anyone call Eric those things? Her father was wrong, so wrong!

She looked around. Shattered pieces of her collection lay strewn about. Her beautiful grotto was now a junk pile. And why? Because of her father! Who was really the savage one? Who was the one incapable of feeling?

Ariel's eyes filled with tears. The grotto became blurry. Flotsam and Jetsam were now two distant shadows moving away. In a moment they would be gone.

"Together forever," they had said. But what if it was a trap? What if Ursula had some sinister plan?

Ariel sighed. She couldn't imagine how her life could be any worse than it was now....

"Wait!" The word flew out of Ariel's mouth before she could think. "I'm coming with you."

Flotsam and Jetsam both turned around. As they smiled, their eyes seemed to pulse with electricity. "Wonderful choice, my dear!" Jetsam said.

As the eels led Ariel out of the grotto, they passed by Flounder and Sebastian.

"Ariel!" Sebastian gasped. "Where are you going? What are you doing with this riffraff?"

"I'm going to see Ursula," Ariel retorted.

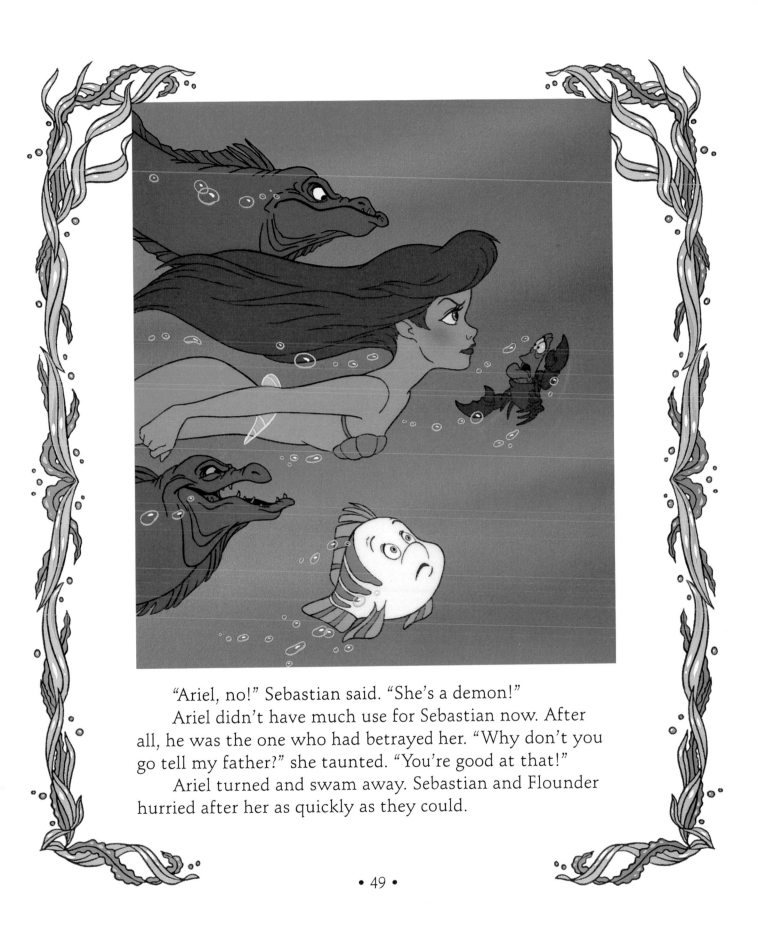

"Ariel, no!" Sebastian said. "She's a demon!"

Ariel didn't have much use for Sebastian now. After all, he was the one who had betrayed her. "Why don't you go tell my father?" she taunted. "You're good at that!"

Ariel turned and swam away. Sebastian and Flounder hurried after her as quickly as they could.

# CHAPTER EIGHT

Ariel hesitated when she reached Ursula's lair. The entrance was the open jaw of an enormous fish skeleton shrouded in puffs of black smoke. The smoke curled around the jaw's pointed fangs.

"This way," Flotsam and Jetsam urged.

Ariel gulped but swam on.

Suddenly something cold and slimy grabbed Ariel's wrist and yanked her downward. She shuddered. It was a shivering, sad-eyed lump, one of many such creatures who moaned and quivered and looked at Ariel with terrified yellow eyes. Gasping with horror, Ariel pulled herself loose.

"Come in, come in, my child," Ursula called.

Ariel spun around. The Sea Witch was leering down at her.

Ariel backed away in fear. This trip didn't seem like such a good idea anymore.

Ursula slid across the seafloor and heaved her massive body toward a vanity table. She admired herself in the mirror and applied lotion to her hair.

"Now then," she began, "you're here because you have a thing for this human, this prince fellow. Not that I blame you. He is quite a catch, isn't he? Well, angelfish, the solution to your problem is simple."

Ursula painted her lips a bright red and gave a twisted smile. "The only way to get what you want is to become a human yourself."

"Can you change me into one?" Ariel asked.

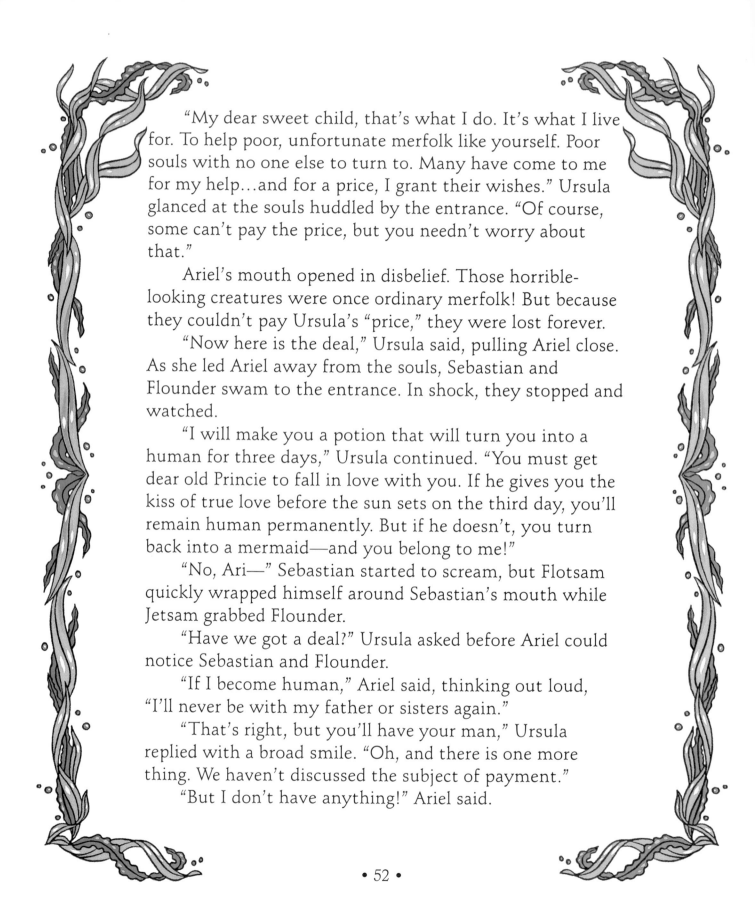

"My dear sweet child, that's what I do. It's what I live for. To help poor, unfortunate merfolk like yourself. Poor souls with no one else to turn to. Many have come to me for my help…and for a price, I grant their wishes." Ursula glanced at the souls huddled by the entrance. "Of course, some can't pay the price, but you needn't worry about that."

Ariel's mouth opened in disbelief. Those horrible-looking creatures were once ordinary merfolk! But because they couldn't pay Ursula's "price," they were lost forever.

"Now here is the deal," Ursula said, pulling Ariel close. As she led Ariel away from the souls, Sebastian and Flounder swam to the entrance. In shock, they stopped and watched.

"I will make you a potion that will turn you into a human for three days," Ursula continued. "You must get dear old Princie to fall in love with you. If he gives you the kiss of true love before the sun sets on the third day, you'll remain human permanently. But if he doesn't, you turn back into a mermaid—and you belong to me!"

"No, Ari—" Sebastian started to scream, but Flotsam quickly wrapped himself around Sebastian's mouth while Jetsam grabbed Flounder.

"Have we got a deal?" Ursula asked before Ariel could notice Sebastian and Flounder.

"If I become human," Ariel said, thinking out loud, "I'll never be with my father or sisters again."

"That's right, but you'll have your man," Ursula replied with a broad smile. "Oh, and there is one more thing. We haven't discussed the subject of payment."

"But I don't have anything!" Ariel said.

"I'm not asking much. Just a token, really. A trifle. You'll never even miss it." Ursula smiled reassuringly. She gave Ariel a gentle touch under the chin. "What I want from you is your voice."

"My...voice?" Ariel couldn't believe her ears.

"That's right; you've got it. No more talking, singing, zip!"

"But without my voice, how can I—"

"You'll have your looks and your pretty face. And you can use body language! Men aren't impressed by conversation. They like women who are demure and quiet."

Ursula proceeded to grab flask after flask of liquid off a shelf and toss them into a cauldron. Ariel watched in fright as pinkish

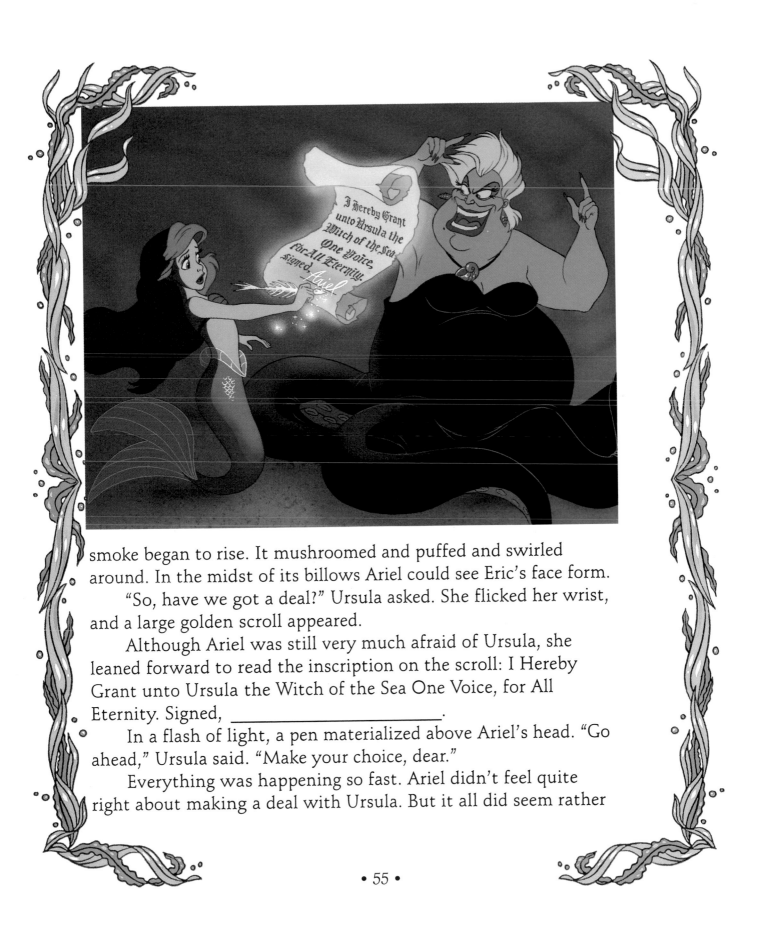

smoke began to rise. It mushroomed and puffed and swirled around. In the midst of its billows Ariel could see Eric's face form.

"So, have we got a deal?" Ursula asked. She flicked her wrist, and a large golden scroll appeared.

Although Ariel was still very much afraid of Ursula, she leaned forward to read the inscription on the scroll: I Hereby Grant unto Ursula the Witch of the Sea One Voice, for All Eternity. Signed, _____.

In a flash of light, a pen materialized above Ariel's head. "Go ahead," Ursula said. "Make your choice, dear."

Everything was happening so fast. Ariel didn't feel quite right about making a deal with Ursula. But it all did seem rather

simple. So, mustering up all her courage, Ariel grabbed the pen and signed her name.

Ursula's eyes glowed with victory. A horrible, wicked smile came across her face. She waved her arms over the cauldron, chanting a magic spell. The smoke swirled like a tornado, and from the cauldron rose two green, smoky hands.

"Now sing!" Ursula commanded.

Ariel obeyed, and as she sang, a bright light began to glow within her throat.

The long green hands reached toward Ariel and plucked the light from her throat.

Ariel's hands instinctively went to her neck. She was no longer making any sounds, but her *voice* was still singing. Her voice was inside the light!

Ursula began to laugh. She held up a seashell locket that hung around her neck and watched in satisfaction as the hands placed the light inside.

Cackling with glee, Ursula waved her hand over the cauldron again. Enormous blasts of smoke shot upward, and a huge orange bubble encircled Ariel.

Ariel flailed desperately. She flipped her tail, trying to swim away. Then, in two flashes of light, her tail was gone. So was the bubble.

She looked down. Where her tail had been, there were now two legs.

Ariel couldn't breathe. She tried to swim, but she was not used to her legs. She felt strangely weighted down. Was *this* what it was like to be human? Was this...drowning?

Sebastian and Flounder broke loose from Ursula's eels. They grabbed Ariel and raced with her toward the surface.

# CHAPTER NINE

Prince Eric sighed. Since his rescue, he hadn't been the same. All he could think about was that girl on the beach.

According to Grimsby, she was just a figment of Eric's imagination.

It was true that Eric hadn't seen her very clearly. He had been too groggy. But there was one thing about her that Eric could never have dreamed up—one thing so beautiful it *had* to be real.

Her voice.

He wanted so badly to hear that girl sing once more. No sound on earth had ever seemed so lovely to him.

Eric picked up his fife and began to play. A sad tune floated across the beach and echoed off the stone wall of his castle.

As the last notes of his song faded away, Eric began walking down the shore. Soon Max was panting along beside him.

Eric tousled the dog's hair and smiled. "Max, I can't get that voice out of my head," he said. "I've looked everywhere for her. Where could she be?"

He paced silently on the sand, hoping against hope he might find her.

Ariel, Sebastian, and Flounder lay exhausted from their swim, on a pile of rocks near where Prince Eric was walking. Ariel slowly lifted her head and blinked in the brightness of the sun. Not too far away, she saw an old shipwreck rotting on the sand. Where was she?

She looked down in the water, just below her feet.
*Feet?*

Ariel lifted one of her legs. She wiggled her toes. What a feeling! She giggled silently.

"Well, look at what the catfish dragged in!" Scuttle landed gently on Ariel's leg and laughed. "Look at you! Look at you! There's something different. Don't tell me. It's your hairdo! You've been using the dinglehopper, right?"

Ariel shook her head.

Scuttle rested a wing on Ariel's toes. "Hmm, I got to admit, I can't put my foot on it right now, but—"

"She's got legs, you idiot!" Sebastian cried out. "She traded her voice to the Sea Witch and got legs!"

"Ariel's been turned into a human!" Flounder chimed

in. "She has three days to make the Prince fall in love with her, and he's got to kiss her."

Ariel couldn't say a word now, but she still felt wonderful. Carefully she tried to stand on her new legs. Boy, did they feel shaky! She didn't know how humans could possibly—

*SPLASH!* She toppled over and landed in the water.

"Just look at her!" Sebastian said. "Oh, this is a catastrophe. Her father is going to kill me! I'm going to march myself straight home now and tell him—"

Ariel lifted him up and shook her head, silently begging Sebastian to change his mind.

"Well, maybe there's still time," Sebastian said, trying to convince Ariel that this was the right thing to do. "If we could get that witch to give you back your voice, you could go home with all the normal fish and just be—" The expression on Ariel's face made him stop. He'd never seen her so sad. With a sigh, he finished his sentence. "Just be miserable for the rest of your life. All right, all right, I'll try to help you find that prince."

Ariel gave Sebastian a kiss. As she lowered him to the rock, he muttered, "Boy, what a soft shell I'm turning out to be."

"Now, let's put some clothing on you," Scuttle said, flying toward the nearby shipwreck. "I'm telling you, if you want to be human, the first thing you have to do is dress like one."

Scuttle pulled a white sail and some rope off the shipwreck and brought them to Ariel, who had waded to shore. She draped the sail around her and tied it in place with the rope.

"You look sensational, kid!" Scuttle said.

Ariel looked at Sebastian and Flounder. Before they could react, a loud sound came over a nearby dune.

"*Arf! Arf!*"

Flounder screamed and dove underwater. Scuttle flew off. Sebastian leapt into a fold of Ariel's costume.

Max came bounding over the dune. He ran to Ariel and began licking her.

"Max! Hey, Max, what's gotten into you, fella?"

It was Eric's voice. Ariel looked toward the dune. And then, in an instant, there he was, looking at Ariel. Max tore himself away and ran toward his master.

"Are you okay, miss?" Eric asked. "I'm sorry if Max scared you. He's really harmless."

Ariel smiled. Eric was so handsome, so gentle. She wished she could say something to him. Instead she blushed and smiled.

"You seem familiar to me," Eric said. "Have we met?"

Max got behind Eric and pushed him closer to Ariel. "We have met!" he said, taking Ariel's hands. "You're the one I've been looking for! What's your name?"

Looking into his eyes, Ariel knew she was in love. Quickly she opened her mouth to say "Ariel," but no sound came out.

"What is it?" Eric asked. "You can't speak?"

Sadly Ariel shook her head.

"Oh, then you can't be who I thought," Eric said, disappointed.

But Ariel was determined not to give up. She began pantomiming what had happened. She pointed to her throat, made swimming motions with her hands, and pretended to pass out. Then she slipped from her rock and fell right into Eric's arms.

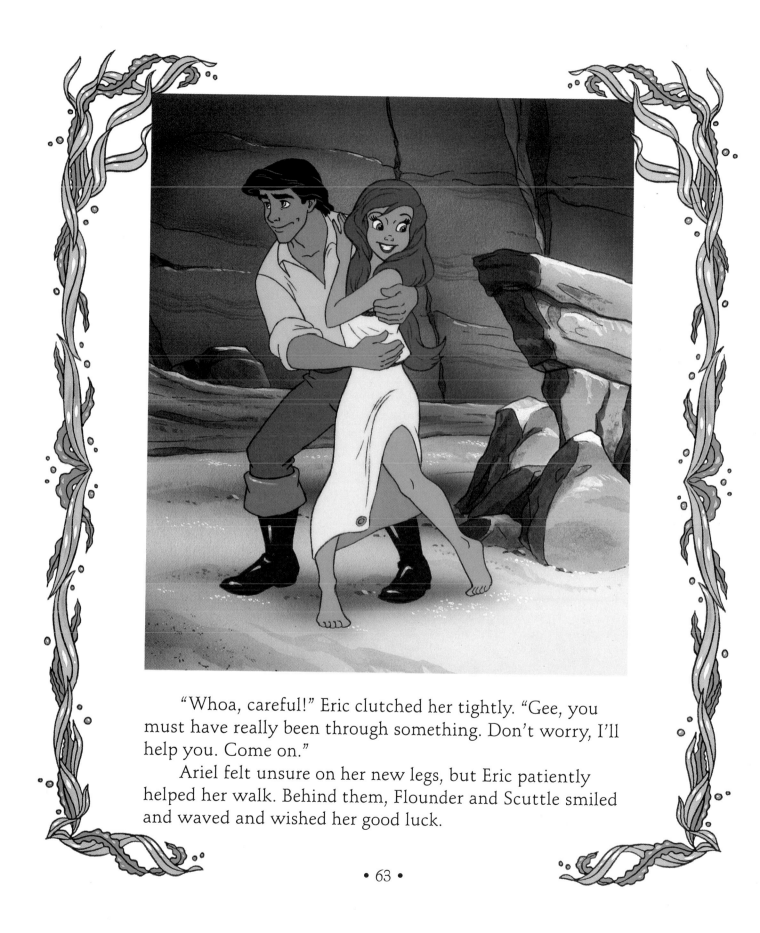

"Whoa, careful!" Eric clutched her tightly. "Gee, you must have really been through something. Don't worry, I'll help you. Come on."

Ariel felt unsure on her new legs, but Eric patiently helped her walk. Behind them, Flounder and Scuttle smiled and waved and wished her good luck.

# CHAPTER TEN

At the castle Ariel was turned over to Eric's housekeeper, Carlotta. Carlotta drew a hot bubble bath for Ariel and sent her sailcloth dress to the washroom. Then she found a lovely pink ball gown for Ariel to wear to dinner.

Sebastian, however, had a very different experience. Hidden in Ariel's sailcloth dress, he traveled to the washroom, where he was dumped into the wash basin. The soapy water made him cough and sputter. He grabbed on to a shirt in the wash, and when one of the housemaids hung the shirt out to dry, Sebastian went with it.

He lifted his head and peered out the shirt pocket. The clothesline was next to an open window in the castle. Sebastian jumped inside, and with a small thump, he landed on a wooden table. He sighed with relief.

Then he saw the knife—a huge knife stuck in the table between two cut-up halves of a fish. Sebastian looked away in horror—and saw two stuffed crabs on a plate.

*Stuffed crabs!*

Sebastian gasped in horror. All around him were creatures from the sea—stuffed, fried, baked, and broiled. And every one of them was very, very dead.

"What is this? I have missed one!"

Sebastian spun around to see the chef. His white apron was stained with blood, and he held a sharp cleaver in his hand.

"Eeek!" Sebastian screamed.

"You are alive?" Holding the cleaver high, the chef came after Sebastian.

With a yelp, Sebastian ran as fast as his claws could carry him.

In the royal dining room Eric stood silently by the window. He watched the sun slowly setting over the water. The table was set, but Ariel had not yet arrived.

Sitting at the table, Grimsby filled his pipe with tobacco. "Eric," he said, "nice young ladies just don't swim around rescuing people in the middle of the ocean."

"I'm telling you, she was real," Eric insisted. "I'm going to find that girl—and I'm going to marry her!"

Carlotta's voice drifted into the room from the hallway. "Come on, honey," she said. "Don't be shy."

Eric turned to see Ariel, looking magnificent in a beautiful gown. Eric was speechless.

Ariel smiled shyly as she walked in.

"Eric, isn't she a vision?" Grimsby said, showing Ariel to her place at the table.

"Uh, you look wonderful" was all Eric could say.

"Comfy, my dear?" Grimsby said. "It's not often we have such a lovely dinner guest, eh, Eric?"

Ariel spotted a fork beside her plate. A dinglehopper, she thought. She grabbed it and began combing her hair.

Eric and Grimsby stared silently. Whoops, Ariel said to herself. Maybe it was bad manners to use a dinglehopper at the table. She quickly put it down.

Grimsby lit his pipe and began to smoke. Ariel stared at the snarfblatt and smiled.

"Uh, do you like it?" Grimsby asked, holding the pipe out with admiration.

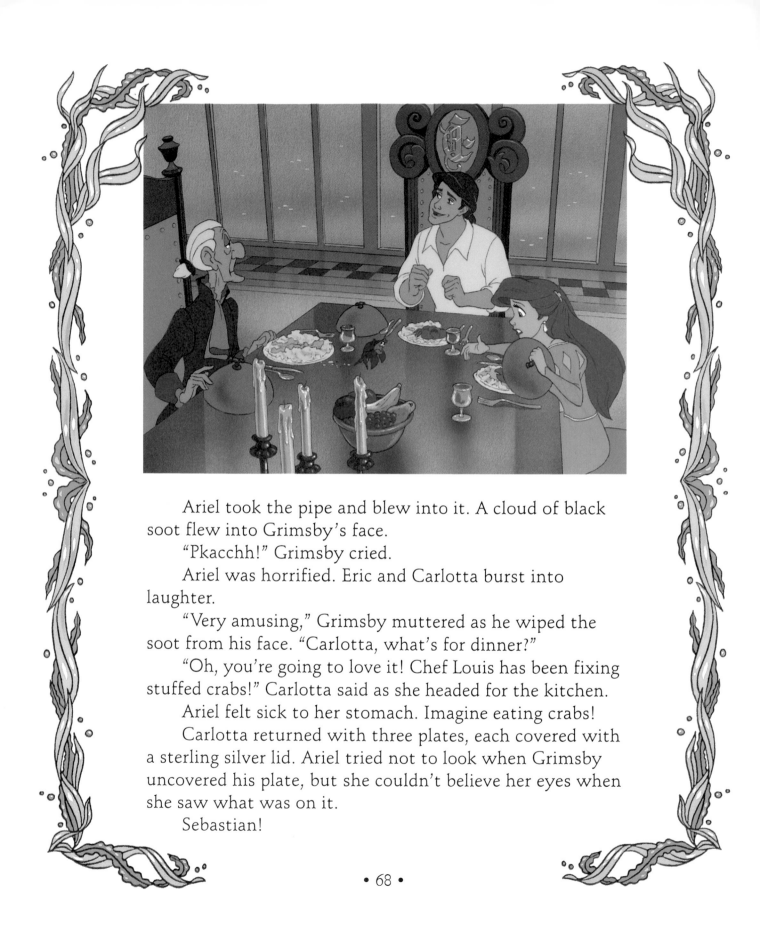

Ariel took the pipe and blew into it. A cloud of black soot flew into Grimsby's face.

"Pkacchh!" Grimsby cried.

Ariel was horrified. Eric and Carlotta burst into laughter.

"Very amusing," Grimsby muttered as he wiped the soot from his face. "Carlotta, what's for dinner?"

"Oh, you're going to love it! Chef Louis has been fixing stuffed crabs!" Carlotta said as she headed for the kitchen.

Ariel felt sick to her stomach. Imagine eating crabs!

Carlotta returned with three plates, each covered with a sterling silver lid. Ariel tried not to look when Grimsby uncovered his plate, but she couldn't believe her eyes when she saw what was on it.

Sebastian!

It was a good thing Ariel had no voice or she would have screamed. She quickly lifted the lid off her plate and gestured for Sebastian to hide there.

"You know, Eric," Grimsby was saying, "perhaps our young guest would like a tour of the kingdom."

Quickly Sebastian skittered across the table and onto Ariel's plate. She slammed the lid closed.

"Well, what do you say?" Eric asked.

Ariel leaned on the lid and nodded with delight.

"Wonderful!" Grimsby said. "Now, let's eat before this crab wanders off my plate...." His voice trailed off. There was only a pile of bread crumbs where his crab should have been.

Ariel breathed a sigh of relief.

So did Sebastian.

That night, Ariel was shown to a splendid guest room. From there she could hear Eric and Max playing in the courtyard. Smiling, she sank into the soft satin sheets of her bed.

On her dresser Sebastian was still picking bits of lettuce and spices from his shell. "This has got to be, without a doubt, the single most humiliating day of my life!" he said. "I hope you appreciate what I go through for you, young lady. Now then, we've got to make a plan to get that boy to kiss you. Tomorrow you've got to look your best. You've got to bat your eyes and pucker up your lips—"

He turned to look at Ariel, but her eyes were already closed. With a shake of his head, Sebastian said tenderly, "You are hopeless, child, you know that?"

Yawning, he walked to the candle and blew it out. Then he curled up next to Ariel on the bed and drifted into a deep sleep.

CHAPTER ELEVEN

Oh, what have I done?" King Triton moaned to himself.

All night long his subjects had been searching for Ariel. Now it was morning, and no one had seen her. They had searched every corner of the seafloor.

None of them suspected the truth. None of them would have thought to look on the land, where Ariel and Prince Eric had just set out for a carriage ride. As they sped over a country bridge, Flounder leapt out of the water below. He spotted Sebastian hiding on the side of the carriage.

"Has he kissed her yet?" Flounder called up.

"Not yet," Sebastian answered.

The tour lasted all day. Ariel fell more in love with Eric every minute. They admired the sights, stopped at a country fair, had a picnic, and danced to an outdoor orchestra. Eric bought her a bouquet of flowers and a beautiful new hat. He even offered her the reins of the carriage. In her enthusiasm Ariel made the horses go so fast that the carriage bounced across a cliff.

That evening, Eric took her on a rowboat across a lagoon. The sunset streaked the clouds with spectacular colors. Sitting in that boat, watching Eric row, Ariel could not imagine a greater happiness.

Nearby, Scuttle sat on a rock and watched. Flounder floated in the water below him. "Nothing is happening! Only one day left, and that boy ain't puckered up once,"

Scuttle said. "This calls for a little vocal romantic stimulation."

Scuttle flew up to the branches of a tree, pushing aside some bluebirds. Clearing his throat, he began to sing: *"BRRAAAWK! CAAAAAW! SKRAAACCKK! EEEEK!"*

Ariel knew who it was right away. She cringed.

"Ow, that's horrible," Eric said. "Somebody should find that poor animal and put it out of its misery."

Hiding at the edge of the rowboat, Sebastian rolled his eyes. "I'm surrounded by amateurs," he said to himself. "If you want something done, you've got to do it yourself!"

He dove into the water and broke off the tip of a long reed. Using it as a baton, he summoned the lagoon animals to attention. "First we've got to create the mood!

"Percussion!" Ducks began tapping a soft drumbeat on turtles' shells.

"Strings!" Grasshoppers rubbed their hind legs together to sound like violins.

"Wind instruments!" Reeds vibrated in the gentle breeze. Together they all played a soft love song.

Sebastian sang in a caressing voice. His words urged Eric to kiss Ariel.

"Do you hear something?" Eric asked.

Ariel could only smile and shrug.

"You know," Eric said, "I feel really bad, not knowing your name. Maybe I could guess. Is it…Mildred?"

Ariel made a face and shook her head.

Eric laughed. "Okay, how about Diana? Rachel?"

As the music continued, Sebastian leapt onto the edge of the boat. He whispered up to Eric, "Her name is Ariel!"

"Ariel?" Eric asked.

Ariel nodded.

"Hmm, that's kind of pretty," Eric said. With a broad smile, he took her hand. "Okay, Ariel."

They floated along, hand in hand, to Sebastian's song. Soon a full moon began to rise over the lagoon. It cast its amber light over the still water. Ariel felt her heart quicken. Eric leaned closer. His smiling face drew nearer. He puckered his lips.

Sebastian grinned. Scuttle wanted to cheer. Flounder flipped his tail with excitement. This was it!

Ariel closed her eyes. She puckered her lips as Eric leaned closer...and closer...and closer...

*SPLASHHHHH!*

The rowboat flipped over, and Ariel and Eric fell into the water. "Don't worry!" shouted Eric. "I've got you!"

All at once, the music stopped. Ducks flew away; turtles ducked underwater. Sebastian groaned. Scuttle and Flounder stared in shock. The romantic mood was broken. The kiss would have to wait for the next day.

Just beneath the rowboat, two shadowy figures laughed. They clasped their tails together, congratulating each other for tipping the boat.

Then, under cover of darkness, as Ursula watched in her crystal ball, Flotsam and Jetsam began to swim home.

"That was a close one," Ursula said to herself. "Too close. At this rate he'll be kissing her by sunset tomorrow, for sure. It's time to take matters into my own tentacles!" From her shelves she pulled a bubbling potion and a glass ball containing a small, delicate butterfly.

She threw the potion and the ball into her cauldron, creating a loud explosion and a big burst of flames.

"Triton's daughter will be mine!" Ursula gloated. "And then I'll make him wriggle like a worm on a hook!"

Ursula cackled. White smoke encircled her. The seashell necklace around her neck began to glow. Over Ursula's laughter, it sang out loud and clear in Ariel's voice.

Then, slowly, Ursula changed. Her enormous body turned slender. Her tentacles became two legs, and her hideous face was transformed into that of a beautiful dark-haired woman.

With a loud thunderclap, Ursula transported herself instantly to the shore near Prince Eric's castle. She waded out of the ocean, singing. To Eric, who was staring out to sea, deep in thought, she appeared at first as a vision. And then, when the glow from Ursula's necklace was reflected in his eyes, she changed into the girl who had saved his life—the one he had been searching for.

The next morning, Ariel awoke to a shout.

"Ariel!"

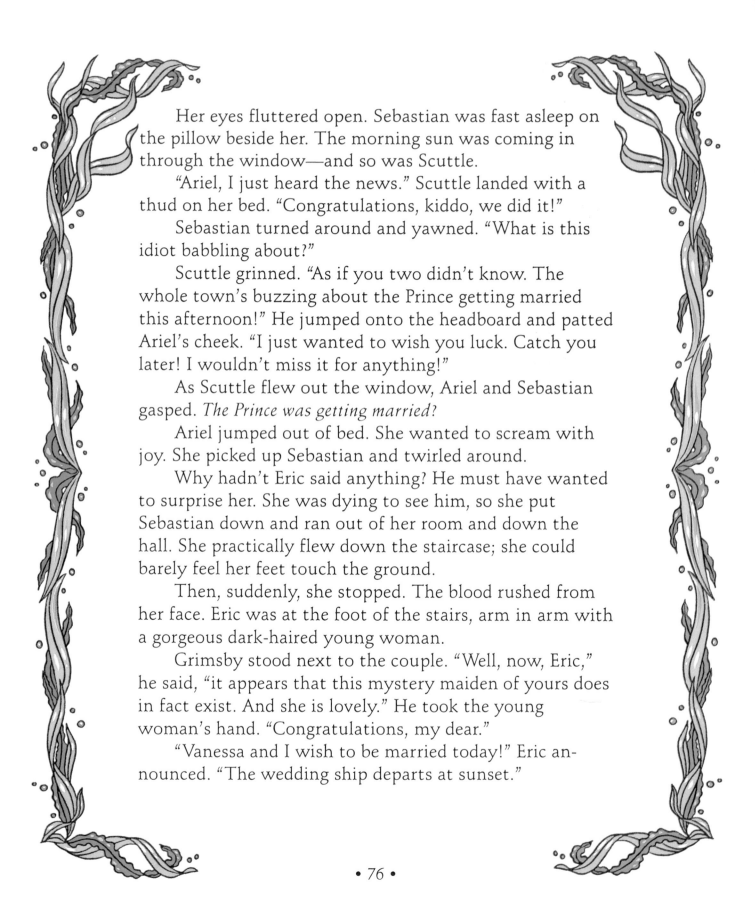

Her eyes fluttered open. Sebastian was fast asleep on the pillow beside her. The morning sun was coming in through the window—and so was Scuttle.

"Ariel, I just heard the news." Scuttle landed with a thud on her bed. "Congratulations, kiddo, we did it!"

Sebastian turned around and yawned. "What is this idiot babbling about?"

Scuttle grinned. "As if you two didn't know. The whole town's buzzing about the Prince getting married this afternoon!" He jumped onto the headboard and patted Ariel's cheek. "I just wanted to wish you luck. Catch you later! I wouldn't miss it for anything!"

As Scuttle flew out the window, Ariel and Sebastian gasped. *The Prince was getting married?*

Ariel jumped out of bed. She wanted to scream with joy. She picked up Sebastian and twirled around.

Why hadn't Eric said anything? He must have wanted to surprise her. She was dying to see him, so she put Sebastian down and ran out of her room and down the hall. She practically flew down the staircase; she could barely feel her feet touch the ground.

Then, suddenly, she stopped. The blood rushed from her face. Eric was at the foot of the stairs, arm in arm with a gorgeous dark-haired young woman.

Grimsby stood next to the couple. "Well, now, Eric," he said, "it appears that this mystery maiden of yours does in fact exist. And she is lovely." He took the young woman's hand. "Congratulations, my dear."

"Vanessa and I wish to be married today!" Eric announced. "The wedding ship departs at sunset."

# CHAPTER TWELVE

How could he?

Ariel kept asking herself that question over and over. Eric had seemed so open, so honest, so kind. And he had been in love with her. She just *knew* it.

She slumped against a pillar on the royal dock. The entire day had passed, and Eric hadn't looked at her even once. It was as if she'd never existed.

Now, under a glorious sunset, Eric's wedding ship was sailing out to sea. Hundreds of people were aboard, laughing and singing. And Ariel had not even been invited.

She buried her head in her arms and began to weep. Alongside her, Sebastian looked on helplessly. From the water below them, Flounder's little sobs floated upward.

At that same moment, Scuttle swooped down over the ship, humming a wedding tune. It would be so exciting to see Ariel get married. He especially wanted to see the bride kiss the groom.

Through a porthole Scuttle could see Ariel fixing her hair and singing. But wait! That dark-haired girl *sounded* like Ariel, but she sure didn't look or act like her.

Scuttle flew closer, and when the girl looked in the mirror, Ursula's reflection looked back out! He heard her say, "Hah! I'll have that little mermaid soon. And when I do, the entire ocean will be mine!"

"The Sea Witch!" Scuttle said to himself.

There was no time to waste. He immediately flew to the dock. "Ariel!" he cried, flustered and out of breath. "I saw the watch—the witch—the witch was watching the mirror and singing in a stolen voice! Do you hear what I'm saying? *The Prince is marrying the Sea Witch in disguise!*"

"Are you sure?" Sebastian said.

"What are we going to do?" Flounder cried.

Ariel sat up. The Sea Witch. She should have known! Ursula had put Eric under a spell.

The sun hovered just above the horizon. Ariel knew that her time was almost up. This was the third day, and she just had to get to Eric before sunset.

Ariel dove into the water. But she'd forgotten that she didn't know how to swim with legs.

Sebastian ran to a row of barrels by the edge of the dock. With his claw, he cut the string that held them together.

The barrels splashed into the water. "Ariel, grab on to one of them!" he called out. "Flounder, take the rope and pull her to the boat! I've got to get to the Sea King. He must know about this."

"What about me?" Scuttle pleaded.

"Find a way to stop that wedding!"

Instantly Scuttle had an idea. He took to the air, and squawking at the top of his lungs, he called out to all the creatures in the area. Bluebirds, flamingos, ducks, seals, dolphins, starfish, lobsters—all of them perked up and followed Scuttle to the wedding ship.

On board the ship, the wedding march had begun. Ursula and Eric were walking down the center of the boat together. Eric's eyes were glazed, his face blank.

Clutching a bouquet of red flowers, Ursula smiled in triumph. The spell was working. Below her chin, the magic

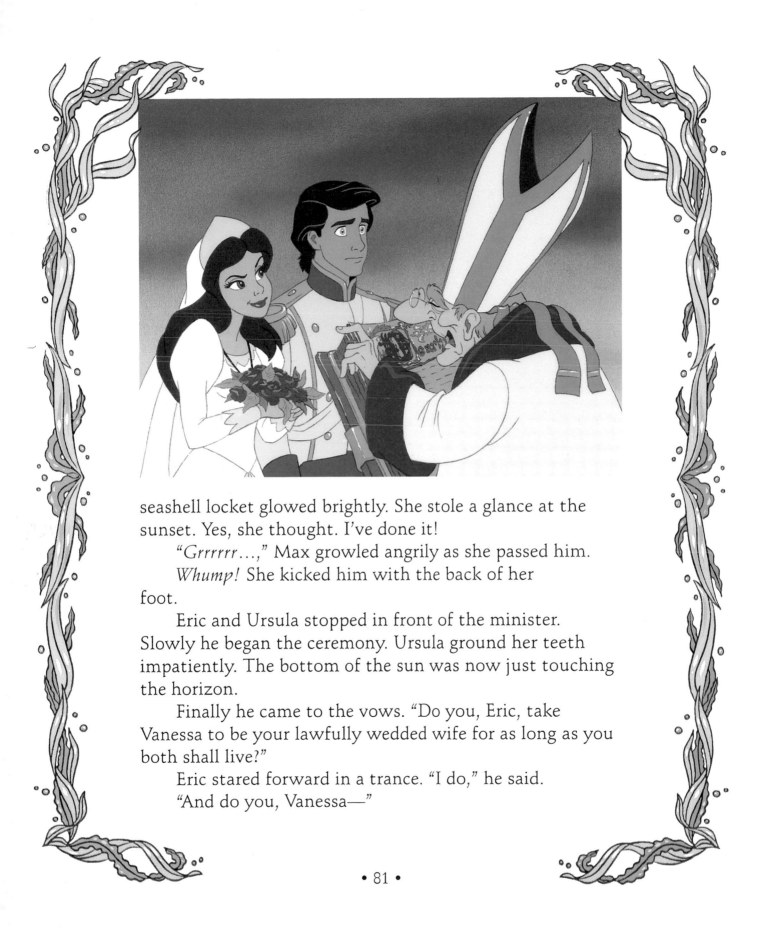

seashell locket glowed brightly. She stole a glance at the
sunset. Yes, she thought. I've done it!

"*Grrrrrr…,*" Max growled angrily as she passed him.
*Whump!* She kicked him with the back of her
foot.

Eric and Ursula stopped in front of the minister.
Slowly he began the ceremony. Ursula ground her teeth
impatiently. The bottom of the sun was now just touching
the horizon.

Finally he came to the vows. "Do you, Eric, take
Vanessa to be your lawfully wedded wife for as long as you
both shall live?"

Eric stared forward in a trance. "I do," he said.

"And do you, Vanessa—"

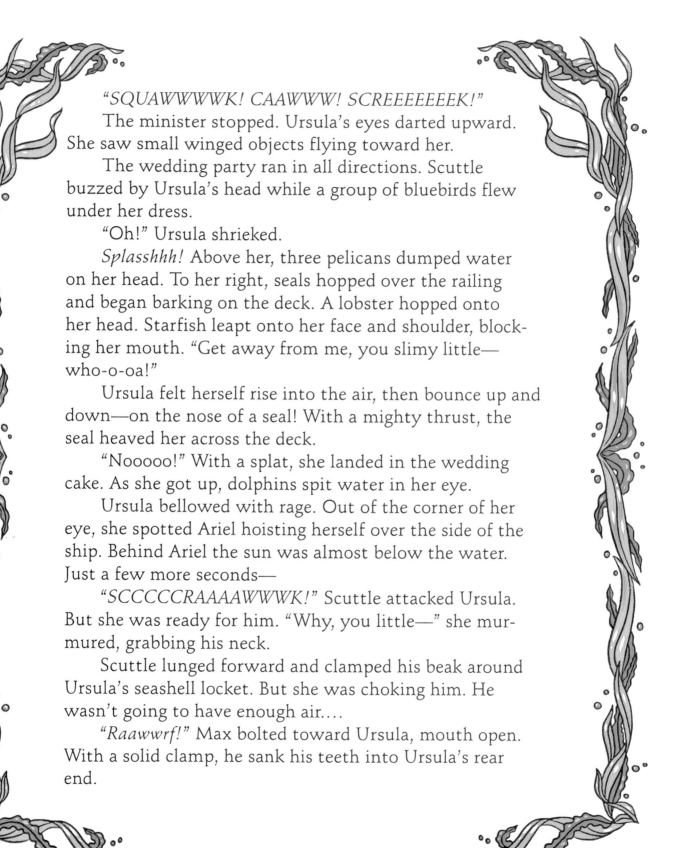

"SQUAWWWWK! CAAWWW! SCREEEEEEEK!"

The minister stopped. Ursula's eyes darted upward. She saw small winged objects flying toward her.

The wedding party ran in all directions. Scuttle buzzed by Ursula's head while a group of bluebirds flew under her dress.

"Oh!" Ursula shrieked.

*Splasshhh!* Above her, three pelicans dumped water on her head. To her right, seals hopped over the railing and began barking on the deck. A lobster hopped onto her head. Starfish leapt onto her face and shoulder, blocking her mouth. "Get away from me, you slimy little— who-o-oa!"

Ursula felt herself rise into the air, then bounce up and down—on the nose of a seal! With a mighty thrust, the seal heaved her across the deck.

"Nooooo!" With a splat, she landed in the wedding cake. As she got up, dolphins spit water in her eye.

Ursula bellowed with rage. Out of the corner of her eye, she spotted Ariel hoisting herself over the side of the ship. Behind Ariel the sun was almost below the water. Just a few more seconds—

"SCCCCCRAAAAWWWK!" Scuttle attacked Ursula. But she was ready for him. "Why, you little—" she murmured, grabbing his neck.

Scuttle lunged forward and clamped his beak around Ursula's seashell locket. But she was choking him. He wasn't going to have enough air....

"*Raawwrf!*" Max bolted toward Ursula, mouth open. With a solid clamp, he sank his teeth into Ursula's rear end.

"*Yeeeaaaaaaaaagghhhhhh!*" Ursula shrieked. She let go of Scuttle. He fell to the deck. The seashell locket hurtled through the air.

Then, with a small clatter, the shell crashed against the deck and broke.

Ariel's voice began to sing. In a golden mist her voice lifted into the air, ringing out over the din, swirling… swirling…

Right into Ariel's throat.

Ariel stood tall and opened her mouth. It was *her* voice again. She let it grow. She gave it all the sweetness and strength she could.

All other sounds stopped. The birds alighted, and the seals and dolphins slipped happily back into the water.

And Eric snapped out of his trance. He shook his head—and when he looked at Ariel, his eyes were alive again. Alive and filled with amazement. But there was something beyond amazement, too, something that could only be love.

"Ariel?" he said, his voice a hoarse whisper.

Ariel felt like bursting with happiness. She cleared her throat. Then she said her first word as a human—the word she had been wanting to say for three days.

"Eric."

"*Arf! Arf!*" Max jumped beside them, barking happily.

"You can talk!" Eric said. "You *are* the one!"

Ursula looked desperately at the sea. The sun had not quite disappeared. "Eric, get away from her!" she shouted.

But her own voice had returned, harsh and scratchy. She put her hand to her mouth in shock.

"It was you all the time!" Eric said to Ariel, taking her hands.

Ariel drew herself closer to him. "Oh, Eric, I wanted to tell you—" She didn't finish. She didn't need to. Eric was leaning down to her. His lips were a breath away from hers. The setting sun gave its final wink of light on the horizon.

"Eric, no!" Ursula cried.

Eric paused for a split second. The sun slipped below the water.

Ariel suddenly went stiff. Pain shot through her. She pulled away from Eric. "Oh!" she gasped.

"You're too late!" Ursula cried triumphantly. "Haaaah-ha-haaah!"

As Ariel slumped to the deck, she saw Eric staring at her legs. She looked down to see that her tail had returned.

*CRRRRACKK!* A bolt of lightning lit up the sky and struck Ursula. She surged with power. Her beautiful slinky body began to swell. It burst out of her wedding dress, a giant mass of blubber and tentacles. Ursula was now herself.

All over the ship, wedding guests shouted and fainted. Roaring with laughter, Ursula made her way across the deck. She wrapped her arm around Ariel and sneered at Eric. "So long, loverboy!" she screeched.

Gripping Ariel tightly, she hoisted herself over the railing and jumped.

As Ariel was pulled into the sea, she could hear Eric shouting her name. And through her panic and fear, she could feel her heart breaking.

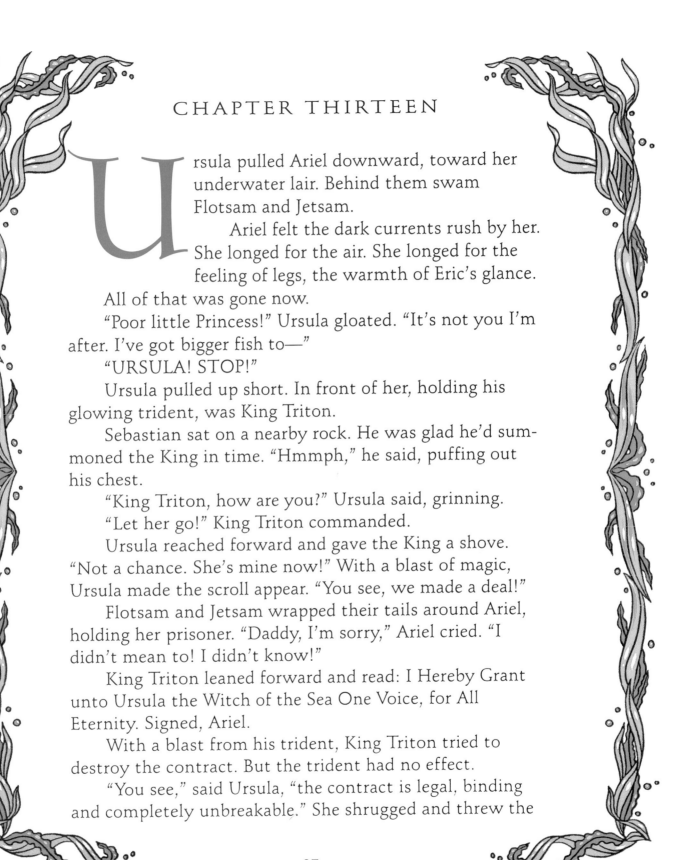

# CHAPTER THIRTEEN

**U**rsula pulled Ariel downward, toward her underwater lair. Behind them swam Flotsam and Jetsam.

Ariel felt the dark currents rush by her. She longed for the air. She longed for the feeling of legs, the warmth of Eric's glance. All of that was gone now.

"Poor little Princess!" Ursula gloated. "It's not you I'm after. I've got bigger fish to—"

"URSULA! STOP!"

Ursula pulled up short. In front of her, holding his glowing trident, was King Triton.

Sebastian sat on a nearby rock. He was glad he'd summoned the King in time. "Hmmph," he said, puffing out his chest.

"King Triton, how are you?" Ursula said, grinning.

"Let her go!" King Triton commanded.

Ursula reached forward and gave the King a shove. "Not a chance. She's mine now!" With a blast of magic, Ursula made the scroll appear. "You see, we made a deal!"

Flotsam and Jetsam wrapped their tails around Ariel, holding her prisoner. "Daddy, I'm sorry," Ariel cried. "I didn't mean to! I didn't know!"

King Triton leaned forward and read: I Hereby Grant unto Ursula the Witch of the Sea One Voice, for All Eternity. Signed, Ariel.

With a blast from his trident, King Triton tried to destroy the contract. But the trident had no effect.

"You see," said Ursula, "the contract is legal, binding and completely unbreakable." She shrugged and threw the scroll over her shoulder. It dissolved into a golden swirl and circled around Ariel.

Quickly Ariel began to shrink. She cried out in agony. Her body was shriveling. She was becoming one of the poor souls in Ursula's collection.

King Triton's eyes were wide with horror. But before he could react, Ursula gave him a sly smile. "Of course, I always was a girl with an eye for a bargain. The daughter of the great Sea King is a precious thing to have. But I might be willing to make an exchange—for someone even better!"

Ariel froze. Her father was staring at her. Sorrow lined his face.

The golden swirl lifted from Ariel and hovered in the water. Within it, the scroll materialized again. "Now, do we have a deal?" Ursula asked.

King Triton pointed his trident toward the scroll. It sent out a blast of gold light. Suddenly Ariel's signature disappeared.

Now, at the bottom of the scroll, it said King Triton.

Ursula threw back her head with laughter. "It's done, then!"

Instantly Ariel grew to normal size. The golden swirl began to settle around the King.

"Oh no!" Ariel screamed. "No!"

Slowly King Triton shrank. His crown fell to the ground.

In seconds all that was left of him was a small quivering lump with big, sad eyes.

Sebastian looked at him in shock. "Your Majesty," he whispered sadly.

"Daddy!" Ariel cried out weakly.

Ursula snatched the crown and put it on. "At last it's mine!" She cackled with her newfound power.

Ariel looked up, away from her father. Her own soul now felt hardened. She had disobeyed her father's strictest rule and fallen in love with a human. She had even made a deal with her father's enemy. And after all that, he had still given his soul to save her.

Ariel felt her blood boil. Hate bubbled up within her. "You!" she snarled at Ursula. "You monster!"

Ursula grabbed the trident and pointed it at Ariel. "Don't fool with me, you little brat! Contract or no, I'll blast—"

*Shhhhhunk!*

A harpoon ripped through one of Ursula's arms. "Yeeeeooooow!" she cried out in pain.

Prince Eric swam above her. "Why, you little fool!" Ursula shouted up at him.

Eric felt as if his lungs were about to burst. He had to go back to his rowboat.

"After him!" Ursula ordered Flotsam and Jetsam.

Eric swam upward and burst through the surface. As he gulped and took in a huge breath of air, Flotsam and Jetsam pulled him back under.

"Come on!" Sebastian shouted to Flounder. They both darted toward Eric. Sebastian pinched Flotsam as hard as he could. Flounder gave Jetsam a whack in the face with his tail.

The eels let go of Eric. But Ursula was prepared. She picked up the trident and aimed it upward. "Say good-bye to your sweetheart!" she said to Ariel.

Ariel grabbed Ursula's hair and pulled. Screaming in pain, Ursula jerked backward. The trident's ray went off

course—and hit Flotsam and Jetsam. With a burst of light, the eels were destroyed.

"My babies!" Ursula cried. "My poor little poopsies!"

Ursula's sadness quickly turned to anger—glowing, steaming anger. Black smoke circled around her.

Ariel swam to the surface. "Eric," she yelled, "you've got to get away from here!"

"No, I won't leave you!" Eric replied.

The sea began to rumble. Eric and Ariel looked down. A gold object rose out of the water and came between them. Ariel felt something solid beneath her, and she and Eric were pushed upward.

Then, like an ancient volcano coming to life, Ursula— a thousand times her normal size—burst through the surface. Ariel and Eric were two mere specks clinging to her crown. Ursula's body cast a shadow that seemed to swallow the sea for miles around.

Ariel and Eric grabbed hands and jumped. "You pitiful fools!" cried the Sea Witch, her voice resounding like a bass drum. Her trident had grown with her, and she swung it high. "Now I am the ruler of all the ocean! The sea and all its spoils must bow to my power!"

The sky cracked with lightning. A wave rose between Eric and Ariel, forcing them apart. "Eric!" Ariel screamed.

Ursula's face was grotesque. Her deep, terrifying laughter boomed out as she swirled the trident in the water.

Eric was drawn into a whirlpool that twisted him violently around. The whirlpool was so powerful, it stirred up the wreckage of an ancient ship from the ocean floor.

Ariel clung to a rock at the bottom of the whirlpool. Above her, in the rapid rush of water, Eric swam toward the shipwreck, grabbed hold, and pulled himself aboard.

The ship's broken mast was jagged and sharp, but its steering wheel was intact. Eric closed his hands around it.

The Sea Witch loomed over the circling waters. She looked down at Ariel and—CRACK!—sent a ray toward her, shattering the rock. Ariel jumped away. She landed on the seafloor, in the dead center of the whirlpool.

"So much for true love!" Ursula thundered. Carefully she pointed her trident at Eric's ship.

Eric gritted his teeth. Ursula's face filled the sky. He swung the steering wheel sharply toward her.

The ship lurched, its mast swung wide—and pierced into Ursula's belly.

"RRRRRRRRAAAWWWWWRRGHH!"

Ursula's cry of pain blotted out the sound of thunder. Giant lightning bolts tore through the sky. As they struck Ursula, she glowed and sizzled. Screaming, she began to sink. Her tentacles lashed out. One of them swiped against Eric's ship and pulled the ship and Eric underwater.

Then, slowly, like a sinking island, Ursula disappeared forever.

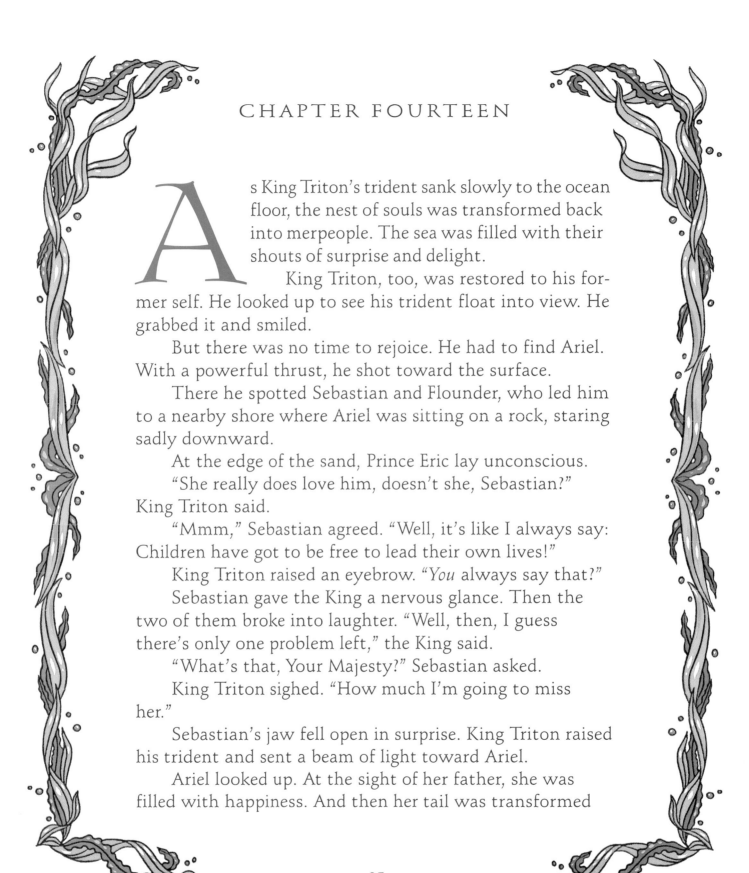

# CHAPTER FOURTEEN

As King Triton's trident sank slowly to the ocean floor, the nest of souls was transformed back into merpeople. The sea was filled with their shouts of surprise and delight.

King Triton, too, was restored to his former self. He looked up to see his trident float into view. He grabbed it and smiled.

But there was no time to rejoice. He had to find Ariel. With a powerful thrust, he shot toward the surface.

There he spotted Sebastian and Flounder, who led him to a nearby shore where Ariel was sitting on a rock, staring sadly downward.

At the edge of the sand, Prince Eric lay unconscious.

"She really does love him, doesn't she, Sebastian?" King Triton said.

"Mmm," Sebastian agreed. "Well, it's like I always say: Children have got to be free to lead their own lives!"

King Triton raised an eyebrow. "*You* always say that?"

Sebastian gave the King a nervous glance. Then the two of them broke into laughter. "Well, then, I guess there's only one problem left," the King said.

"What's that, Your Majesty?" Sebastian asked.

King Triton sighed. "How much I'm going to miss her."

Sebastian's jaw fell open in surprise. King Triton raised his trident and sent a beam of light toward Ariel.

Ariel looked up. At the sight of her father, she was filled with happiness. And then her tail was transformed

into two legs, and suddenly she was wearing a gorgeous blue dress.

Ariel was human again—this time for good.

Eric began to stir. He sat up, held his head, and looked around. Then he saw Ariel coming toward him out of the ocean.

A smile lit up Eric's face. He ran to Ariel and swept her up in an embrace.

They were free. They belonged to each other.

And finally, they shared a long, long kiss.

To this day, the merpeople still talk of Ariel and Eric's wedding. They tell of the glorious cake and the grandness of the wedding ship. And no one will ever forget King Triton's wedding present.

After Ariel and her father shared a tight embrace, King Triton waved his trident in a great arc, and a dazzling rainbow appeared in the sky. It expressed Triton's hope that the young couple would have a brilliant, colorful future. And they did.